VAMPZOMPOCALYPSE

ROBIN REED

Cover by Mike Dominic.

ISBN: 978-0-9899248-1-8

CHAPTER ONE

ÉDUARD DODGED PIKACHU, SIDE-STEPPED OPTIMUS Prime, and almost collided with the late Charles Manson. He really wished he was at home, staying in like any other sane resident of West Hollywood. But, there was no blood in the fridge because Larthia and he had both forgotten the holiday was coming up. By the time they remembered, on the afternoon of Halloween, there was nothing left.

"Are you really going out?" Larthia asked as Éduard opened the door. "We usually Buffy it on Halloween. Besides, Gary and Lazarko are coming over."

It was true that vampires usually laid low on Halloween. Éduard knew the vampire who was technical consultant on *Buffy the Vampire Slayer* and had told that fact to Joss Whedon.

"I'm starving, Larthia, and you told me the delivery place can't get through the crowds."

"Good luck." She looked out the window at the costumed humans filling Santa Monica Boulevard so thickly the street wasn't visible. "And bring me one."

The West Hollywood Halloween street party attracted over four hundred thousand partiers every year, filling the streets with people in every possible costume, from Mickey Mouse to BB-8, and some that were not possible, conveying concepts rather than characters. Éduard ducked to avoid a woman dressed as Existential Dread and then ducked the other way to avoid bumping into the Bechdel Test.

Many costumes were highly revealing, on both men and women. More on men, perhaps. West Hollywood was famous for its gay population.

To blend in, Éduard wore his *Interview With the Vampire* best, lace at his cuffs and all. He liked the understated look of Louis more than the flashy Lestat. In this crowd, he was underdressed. The entire band Devo passed him, with their upside-down pyramid hats, then vampire Marilyn Monroe went the other way. Not a real vamp, Éduard knew all the locals.

Santa Monica Boulevard was a very wide street between La Cienega and San Vicente, but costumed bodies filled it with little room to spare. The air vibrated to the sound of bands performing on nearby stages, and the shouts of conversations of all the partiers. Éduard wanted to be at home, watching *Fright Night*, or *The Lost Boys*, on the couch with Larthia.

Blood surrounded him, contained in sacks called humans. Warm, tasty, nourishing blood. He could grab any one of them, bite and be satisfied. With this many people around him, no one would notice. He rarely drained a victim completely; he would just leave a dazed costume-wearer lying on the street. Everyone would assume he or she was drunk or high. It would be easy. Especially since a good percentage of the crowd was indeed drunk or high.

Usually Éduard was careful not to leave any evidence or

witnesses but who would think anything was strange in this circumstance? He chose a devil woman and reached to take her arm. Before he could, a man in a business suit bumped into her, then leaned forward and opened his mouth.

"What are you doing, freak?" the woman said. Both the man's hands grabbed her, hard enough that she couldn't pull away.

"Hey there, sir, you're hurting the lady." Éduard had been planning to drink her blood, but he saw no reason for this rough treatment.

The man bit her on one arm. Did they know each other? Was this pre-arranged? In the kinky town of West Hollywood, many things were possible. She screamed, and her agony did not seem pre-arranged. The man lifted his head and a strip of flesh came away, clenched in his teeth. Blood flowed down the woman's arm, blending with her red makeup.

Éduard always said that what adults did together was their business, as long as it was consensual. Somehow, flesh-eating seemed like it was probably not, especially on the part of the person being eaten.

He took hold of the man and tried to pull him away from the woman. At first he didn't use his full strength, not wanting to tear the human apart. The fellow didn't look at Éduard, he just kept biting. The devil woman fell to her knees, still screaming.

The costumed crowd moved around them both, no one noticing what was going on. "You must release her, sir," Éduard said as he put both hands on the man and pulled. This finally got the attention of the business-suited human, who moved both eyes toward the vampire but otherwise showed no expression. He opened his mouth wide and bit Éduard on the right hand.

Shock and surprise made Éduard react with the full extent of his vampire strength. He pulled his hand away, which caught on the lower jaw, ripping it free of the man's face. The jaw flew away into the crowd.

Tongue flapping free, blood pouring down the front of his suit, the man finally looked like he belonged at a Halloween party. He lunged at Éduard and tried to bite again, which was impossible with no lower teeth.

Larthia had turned Éduard in 1813, when Napoleon ruled France. He had seen many strange things since then, but a jawless man with his tongue loose and no sign of a soul in his eyes, had not presented itself to his sight in all those years. There was no way this human was alive, the vampire thought, but neither did he display the normally dormant characteristics of the dead.

As for the undead, there was no variety that Éduard had experienced that could explain what he saw. The man was more like the silly, fictional creatures that paraded through so much popular media these days. Éduard considered them low-rent undead, with no subtlety and no passion. Plus, they paid no attention to their appearance. He much preferred a well-dressed, seductive vampire to the messy things that had taken over the popular consciousness.

The biggest reason why the man in front of him couldn't be what he seemed to be was that they weren't real. Éduard had never heard of any instance of them being anything other than the fevered imaginings of screenwriters and hack novelists.

Without a word, the jawless man argued for his reality when many others of his kind appeared behind him. Screams ran through the crowd, as costumed party-goers turned and ran, though there was no room to run. Humans in costumes started biting every limb, torso or head they could sink their teeth into. Kylo Ren ripped his mask off and bit Strawberry Shortcake. Godzilla was assaulted by Dangermouse. The crowd surged back and forth, no one able to escape in the press of thousands of bodies, each one biting or being bitten.

Éduard fought his way toward the side of the street, not sparing his strength. He punched The Incredible Hulk, his fist piercing the green man's face and emerging from the back of his skull. The vampire pulled three of the legs off the giant spider Shelob, a spray of blood revealing that one of them contained a human arm. There was no way to tell which costume contained a living human and which the undead, so he pushed his way through them all, ripping and tearing through the wall of bodies. He had to find a place where he could escape.

A brief moment with a clear space around him allowed Éduard to lift himself above the crowd. It was not accurate that vampires could fly, exactly, but they could lessen the pull of gravity on themselves in order to jump high, like astronauts on the moon. He sailed above the crowd and began to run, placing each foot carefully on a head then pushing off. This took him toward the north side of the street. If he could reach a building he could climb to the safety of a roof.

A two-headed troll stood tall, the costumed human looking over the heads of the crowd, also seeking escape. Eduard aimed for the head that seemed to contain an actual skull inside it but misjudged. His foot fell on the head made of cardboard. The head collapsed, dropping Éduard into the roiling mass of bodies once again.

Kicked and stepped upon by many feet, Éduard bounced through the crowd and ended up with his face planted on the concrete of the sidewalk. A man who looked like Willy

Wonka leaned over and held out his hand. Finally, someone who was willing to help others, even in this extreme circumstance.

The top hat fell off as the man leaned closer, revealing that his left eye had been torn out. He opened his mouth to bite. Éduard tried to push himself back, but there was no room with all the of the panicked crowd. Nearby, Vampirella crawled on all fours with her intestines dragging on the pavement.

Willy Wonka stopped and sniffed, looked confused, then began to stand up. He seemed to abandon the attempt to eat Éduard. Before the vampire could wonder why, Wonka was attacked by a large fur-bearing animal. The snarls of the predatory creature competed with the screams of the humans.

The animal's tail waved in Éduard's face, obscuring what was happening. A moment later the creature turned to face Éduard, holding the severed head of Willy Wonka in the air. He dropped the head after a moment and held out his paw to the vampire. "Let us go," he said in a thick Russian accent.

This was no costumed human. It was a wolf, with real fur and a real stench. One gold canine tooth gleamed. Many gold chains adorned his neck. Éduard knew him. He let the wolf pull him to his feet.

They were close enough to the closed storefronts that Éduard thought he could jump and grab features on the walls and get to the roof. "I can jump, what about you?"

The wolf grunted. "Get me started."

"Hang on." With the wolf holding him around the neck, Éduard jumped at his maximum low gravity and got a hand around a piece of metal sticking out of the wall. The wolf scrambled over him and kept going up. The vampire found several more handholds and soon reached the roof.

"Thanks, Lazarko."

"No problem," the wolf said as his form shifted and a man in his fifties with thick dark hair took his place. His canine tooth was still gold and he still had many gold chains around his neck. Somehow, and Éduard never knew how, he was clothed when he changed back, always in a garish striped suit, with no tie. "I see you dancing on heads, then fall," he said.

Éduard turned to look at the crowd he had just escaped. Screams still filled the air. Bodies, both moving and not, in every possible and some impossible costumes, covered the entirety of Santa Monica Boulevard. Blood ran through the gutters.

Éduard didn't often engage in English profanity, he felt French had some much more elegant expressions for every occasion, but this time he felt only one word would do. "Just what the fuck is going on down there?"

"Zombies," said Gary the Gay Ghost from behind him.

CHAPTER TWO

"ARE YOU SURE, GARY?" ÉDUARD TURNED TO FACE THE ghost. So did the werewolf, who did not seem happy to see him.

"Sure." Gary was translucent, a little hard to see in the dark of the night, but clear enough that Éduard could make out his bare chest under a vest, and tight pants. His hair was cut very short. "It's all over the news," he said. "Straight up Romero zombies, *Night of the Living Dead* standard issue."

"But they're not real," Éduard objected.

"They are now."

"Fast zombies or slow zombies?" Lazarko asked.

Gary rolled his eyes. "I said *Night of the Living Dead,* wolfman."

"I like fast. You can run away from slow ones, easy."

"Are we really going to have this conversation?" Éduard asked. "With real ones down there eating people?"

"I just say, slow is no good."

"But they're everywhere, Lazarko. No matter how far you run, there are more there."

"I can run very far, especially as wolf. No one eat my

brains."

"Okay, okay. What are we going to do now?" Éduard said.

"The brains thing is from *Return of the Living Dead*," Gary said. "John Russo, Romero's co-writer on '*Night*' had the right to make sequels so he started his own series."

"Gary!" Eduard said. "I want to get home and see if Larthia is safe."

"Sorry." The ghost looked embarrassed, or as embarrassed as a ghost can look.

The high-rise that Éduard called home rose above the fray. Lights were on in many of the condos, and out in quite a few. Éduard looked up, trying to figure out how to get there without going down to street level. Balconies outside each condo seemed like the best route.

"You watch *The Walking Dead*?" Lazarko asked. "My wife like. Me not so much. They eat brains." He stuck his arms out and imitated a zombie. "Braaaaaains."

"What? No," Gary almost shouted. "I mean, they eat all parts of human bodies, but they don't go around saying 'Brains' like in the '*Return*' films."

Éduard just shook his head and let them talk.

"I could eat that Darryl up, in a different way if you know what I'm saying," Gary added.

"Ah, don't talk to me of such things," the Russian werewolf said. "Lazarko is real man!"

"Your wife probably had you fixed at the vet," Gary muttered.

"I hear! I rip you apart if you are solid!"

"Shut up," Éduard said." I'm going to try for the lowest balcony and climb from there."

A long jump to the top of a delivery truck, then several more, touching down on cars, took Éduard to his building. Lazarko stayed pretty close behind, in wolf form again.

Costumed zombies tried to grab his ankles in a few places but he got past them easily. He turned his head to stare when he saw the Dragonball Z guy, whose name he could never remember, gnawing on the leg of a screaming female Ghostbuster. She looked like the Melissa McCarthy one.

The only place to land next to the building was street level. As soon as Éduard did, zombies turned and started toward him. Lazarko landed next to him.

"I don't think I can lift you to the first balcony."

"Is all right. See you at your place." Lazarko bounded off toward the building entrance. Éduard looked up and leapt, grabbing a metal strut under the balcony. From there it was an easy climb for a vampire. He lived on the fourteenth floor, though, so it took a while.

Gary floated up to him as he climbed. "Hey, Ed."

"Gary."

"The wolfman is wrong about slow zombies."

"I agreed with you back there." Éduard pulled himself up to the third-floor balcony. The curtains of the condo were closed.

"Unless he means 28 Days Later, but they aren't really zombies."

"You don't say."

"They're living, but they have this virus."

Éduard grunted as jumped toward the next floor. "Maybe these aren't like any movie."

"I watched the news for a while before I went out to see for myself. They seem like standard Romeros, as I said."

"Good to know." Grasping the railing of the eighth-floor balcony, Éduard heard a growl. He pulled his head up to look and saw a naked, bald, fat man staring at him. A rope of saliva hung from the man's lips as he moaned and opened his mouth.

It was Mr. Palmerstein. Éduard didn't know him well, but they nodded when they saw each other in the lobby. He was a former exec at Fox, and had been involved in an age discrimination lawsuit with the studio. He lost, but he still talked about it every chance he got.

Right now, Mr. Palmerstein seemed more interested in advancing on Éduard with the intent to bite him. Then he stopped, looked confused, and turned away.

"I don't think they like the smell of vampire," Gary said, floating a few feet away from the balcony.

"The first one I met bit me hard." Éduard's hand still throbbed from the wound. He pulled himself up and stood near the naked zombie.

"Really? I wonder if you'll turn. We can call you a zomvamp."

"That's ridiculous. I'm already dead. Besides, I prefer vampzom."

"We'll see."

Éduard looked at the zombie. "I hate to leave him like that. He was an okay guy."

Gary shrugged his incorporeal shoulders. "Shot to the head should work."

"Do you think I carry a gun? This isn't *Underworld*." Éduard looked around. There was a barbeque and two lawn chairs. He picked up one of the chairs and dismantled it. A section of aluminum pole looked strong enough. He hefted it, then noticed a curtain being pulled back behind the glass door. Mrs. Palmerstein peered out.

Éduard couldn't think of anything to do but smile and wave, as he did when he saw her in the lobby or halls. He had never spoken a word to the woman.

"Do it," she said, loudly enough to be heard through the door.

"Excuse me, ma'am?"

"You heard me, Mr. Forrier. He attacked me and I pushed him out there. Finish him off."

"You do know what he is, Mrs. Palmerstein. What I have to do."

"Course I do. I met him on a zombie picture. Nineteen eighty two. *Hot Wet Prison Riot of the Dead.* A women's prison zombie picture. I was the leader of one of the prison gangs. I was a looker in those days. It did well in drive-ins."

"So it's all right if I push this pole through his head."

"Go ahead. He's a cheap bastard anyway."

Éduard used all his strength to impale Mr. Palmerstein's head with the pole. The naked zombie looked surprised, then fell to the ground.

"Thanks." The curtain closed.

The rest of the balconies didn't offer any zombies to kill. Éduard saw a family watching TV. They didn't see him. He got to the fourteenth floor, Gary rising serenely next to him. He knocked on the glass door. Larthia had closed the heavy blackout drapes.

A minute later the curtains were pulled aside and Larthia looked out. "Éduard!" She opened the door. "What are you doing out there?"

"You know Gary the Gay Ghost," Éduard said as he entered the apartment. "We should have another guest soon, if he makes it."

"Yes, of course, Gary. Can I get you some coffee? Or snacks?"

"I don't eat or drink, Mrs. Forrier."

"Of course, I forget." Larthia was a small woman with dusky skin. She wore a simple black dress, not a costume because she had not gone out to the party. Éduard met her in 1813, but she was much older than that. She was born in the Etruscan city of Tarchna, before Rome existed.

Someone pounded on the front door. "There's our other guest," Éduard said. He moved to the door and opened it. A blood covered wolf staggered in. "Shut door!" Lazarko growled. Éduard looked out and saw a group of his neighbors lurching toward him, moaning and with their mouths open. Except Graham Tenderweil, a third chair viola player for the LA Symphony, who lived just down the hall and had no face at all. The vampire closed the door and locked all the locks. He hoped that would be enough.

"Had to fight...all way upstairs." Lazarko swiftly became human, though still blood covered. Parts of his suit were torn. How did that happen? Éduard thought. He noticed something else.

"You have something on your lapel."

"What? Here?" Lazarko brushed the front of his suit but didn't get it.

"To your left."

"Here?" The wolfman missed it again.

"Further down."

"Ah!" Lazarko picked the offending object off his suit. "What is?"

"I think it's Graham Tenderweil's nose."

"Very good." Lazarko threw the severed facial feature into his mouth and chewed.

Larthia hugged Éduard tight. "What is happening out there?"

"Have you seen the news?" Éduard asked.

"No, I've been watching *The Vampire Diaries* marathon on cable."

Gary cleared his throat, though how he did was another mystery. "Ed? Zombie apocalypse?"

"Right." Éduard found the remote and turned on the TV. He didn't have to change the channel many times before he found footage of zombies chowing down on humans.

"This is Bonnie Berdlinger with KTLA news in Silverlake." Bonnie was a blond in a tight dress, but to be fair, Éduard thought she was more than a typical news bimbo. She handled traffic deaths, fatal shootings, and murder-suicide scenes with professionalism, intelligence, and a big smile. She stood on a street corner, people running in all directions behind her. "There are continuing reports of people biting other people - "

A tall man in a biker vest ran into the picture and bit into Bonnie's head. He pulled a strip of her scalp away, hair clinging to it, with his teeth. Soon the picture wavered as the cameraman was also attacked. The screen went black.

"You know I don't like zombie movies, darling," Larthia said.

Éduard changed channels again. And again. The news was the same on CNN, MSNBC, and Fox News, where an interview guest ate Sean Hannity. "At least there's some good news," Gary said.

"These aren't movies, Larthia." He put down the remote. He walked to the balcony door and pulled open the curtains. When he opened the door the sound of screams came from the street. Larthia moved, looking shocked. On the balcony she stood by Éduard's side and watched the chaos.

"Oh my."

Gary and Lazarko also looked out over the railing.

"It's - it's real, isn't it?" Larthia looked down, unable to take the horror any more.

"*Vampire Diaries*, huh." Gary closed his eyes and smiled. "I sure could go for Damon. Rowwr."

CHAPTER THREE

"IT IS THE END OF THE WORLD," LAZARKO GROWLED.

Larthia lifted her head, looking solemn. "He's right."

"It's rare you agree with Lazarko, darling," Éduard said.

"Hmm? Oh, I meant Gary's right. Damon is a hunk."

The group retreated into the apartment and locked the balcony door. Éduard rubbed the hand that had been bitten. It hurt, which was strange. Usually wounds healed within minutes. He also realized that he was very hungry. He hadn't had any blood when he went out and there was still none in the fridge.

"What are we going to do?" asked Larthia.

"I think we're safe enough in here," Éduard said. "Surely it will die down and the authorities will fix it."

"That's what they say on *Fear the Walking Dead*," Gary said, "but the authorities never come."

"What do they do to survive?" Larthia asked.

Gary looked a little sheepish. "I don't know, I only watched one episode and crapped out. It's just not the same as *The Walking Dead*."

"We're safe here." Éduard tried to sound cheerful. "I have triple security locks on the door."

The door rattled and the sound of hands beating on it came into the apartment.

"Move furniture!" Lazarko shouted. The two vampires and the wolfman pushed two bookcases and a tall shelving unit with knick-knacks on it in front of the door. The ghost supervised. "It's not even," he said when they finished. "It makes the décor look unbalanced."

"We're trying to survive the zombie apocalypse, not redecorate." Éduard put a hand on the shelving unit to steady it.

"Civilized people can do both," Gary sniffed. "Say, Ed, you don't have a single book on these bookcases."

"Books aren't really my thing. I only learned to read after becoming a vampire."

Gary floated closer to the bookcases. "What are these? Geez, you still have VHS tapes?"

On the TV, tourists who had retreated to the top of the Eiffel Tower fell off the iconic structure while trying to escape being turned into French cuisine.

"Some of these never came out on DVD." Éduard sounded defensive. "Besides, live as long as I have and you'll learn not to follow all the latest fashions, even in video technology."

The streets of Manila were a buffet.

"I have DVDs and Blu-Rays too," Éduard said. "I went through a Laser Disk period, I have those in storage. Don't get me started on BetaMax and HD DVD."

A poor neighborhood in Johannesburg exploded with gunfire. The army tried to hold off a tide of lurching corpses that wouldn't stop.

"All vampire movies? No love stories? No action?" Lazarko turned to Larthia. "You have anything to eat?"

"Oh, yes, I laid in some snacks for you, since you're the only one who eats."

"Please."

Larthia went to get the snacks.

The famous streetcars of San Francisco couldn't move. Guts and brains fouled the cables that pulled them.

"I have some non-vampire stuff, but it's hard to care about the drama of mortals when I know they're going to die soon anyway." Éduard pulled out a VHS tape.

Contact was lost with St. Petersburg when the TV station was overrun with chomping hordes.

"This is the first movie with the word 'vampire' in the title. *The Vampire of the Coast. 1913.* Nothing to do with vampires like me, it's about a gang of robbers."

"Some of the early movies that used the word 'vampire,'" Larthia said as she brought in wings and beef jerky, "were about women who seduced men, not blood suckers. I was an extra in a couple of those."

Éduard cast a glance at the food and wished he could eat them. He needed to get some blood soon. Lazarko wolfed the meaty snacks down. Lazarkos's blood, his life, smelled so good. Éduard already had the zombie virus or whatever in him. Would drinking Lazarko's blood turn him into a vampzomwolf?

"You have a whole Hammer Films section," Gary said admiringly. "I see everything from *The Brides of Dracula* to *The Legend of the Seven Golden Vampires.*"

"Of course; everything I could find, vampires, mummies, Frankenstein, even their non-horror."

The images on the TV finally caught Éduard's attention. Corpses being pushed into a mass grave by bulldozers flowed like water down the side of the massive hole in the ground.

"Look," Éduard said. "That is truly horrible."

"Reminds me of something," Gary said.

"*World War Z!*" they both said together.

"And Brad Pitt's divorced so he's back on the market," Gary said with a big smile.

Larthia looked troubled and pulled Éduard aside. "Darling, if these zombies are truly everywhere, don't you see what it means for us?"

"We'll have to stay in the house for a while, until things get back to normal."

"More than that, I'm afraid. Where are we going to get blood?"

Éduard's stomach growled at the thought. "There have to be fresh humans out there somewhere."

"Can we drink zombie blood?"

Éduard made a face. "That would be like sucking on a corpse. You know it's not the blood itself but the life, the essence."

"Do you want to hunt for the last few living humans, who are hiding from zombies? We like to go to bars and clubs, pick up an easy meal and dance the rest of the night away."

Larthia had a point. Vampires generally like civilization. Many lived in crowded cities, where food is plentiful and easy to catch. He still didn't want to be too alarmist.

"Remember the big wars last century? We scavenged the not-quite-dead on the battlefields and still made it to our favorite sidewalk café in Paris every night."

Larthia looked grim. "Humans call this the zombie apocalypse for a reason. Living blood will be hard to find. Vampires will fight over the last few humans."

It couldn't be that bad, could it? Éduard thought. He had never thought of zombies as rivals for his food supply.

"You could be right, dearest," Éduard said. "But there's really nothing we can do. We might as well have a vampire movie marathon and see what happens."

"What if the power goes out?"

"What?"

"Humans run the power grid. It always fails in apocalypse movies."

This was a staggering thought. He wouldn't be able to watch any of his beloved movies or TV shows? He couldn't make blood smoothies? He couldn't post in the Vampires of LA Facebook group? "This is serious," he said. "We must do something."

Gary and Lazarko argued over what movie to watch as Éduard moved toward them, mind reeling with the dire possibilities.

"I feel like a comedy," Gary stated. "*Love at First Bite,* or *What We Do in the Shadows.*"

Lazarko waved his right hand, which clutched a Blu-Ray case. "No, I'm in mood for classics. *Dracula,* maybe, or *Vampyr.*"

"That old stuff is boring." Gary looked up as Éduard came toward him. "Hey Ed, why don't you have many zombie movies? We could watch *Shaun of the Dead.*"

"Gentlemen," Éduard announced. "My dear companion of over two centuries has made me realize there is more at stake than what movie we watch."

The ghost and the werewolf looked blank.

"If this is a real apocalypse, won't you miss civilization? Lazarko, you have a business, you like being a big shot in the Russian community in West Hollywood. And, occasionally eating someone." Lazarko nodded. "Gary– well, you like to hang out with the living."

Gary rolled his translucent eyes. "Ghosts are such dreary company. Moaning. Rattling chains. It gets old."

"Well then. Larthia and I have decided we should do something about the current situation."

"Like what?" Lazarko asked.

"Um." Éduard turned to Larthia. "What were you thinking of, dear?"

"Call the vampire council."

"There really is a vampire council?" Gary sounded amused.

"Sure," Éduard said. "There's a local one, regional, and national. A whole vampiric government."

"I never hear you mention this."

"It's kinda secret. We really shouldn't have told them, Larthia."

"The by-laws allow it in an emergency. Wouldn't you call this an emergency?"

"I don't know, they put a vampire to death who told a human about the council during the black plague."

"That was different, the human was the Pope. People tend to believe the Pope."

"Well, the vampire also told the Pope that fire would keep the disease away. Poor Clement sweated for months in a room full of torches."

"Did they use pleasant-smelling herbs to cover the smell of sweat?" Gary asked. Everyone looked at him. "Pope-pourri?"

"If you had flesh I would eat you for that," Lazarko growled.

"Anyway." Éduard took his iPhone out of a pocket in his eighteenth-century style vest and dialed the secret vampire council number in his contacts.

"L.A. Vampire Council," a nasal female voice answered.

"Hey, Sylvia, Éduard Forrier here. Is anyone there?"

"The next meeting is scheduled for Friday at midnight."

"I thought maybe there would be an emergency meeting," Éduard said.

"Really? Why?"

"The zombies?"

"I know you like movies, Ed, you watching a Halloween zombie marathon?"

"For real, Sylvia. Turn on a TV."

"No TV allowed in the council chambers."

Éduard knew the rule. Except for the landline phone Sylvia was using, all electronic devices were banned in the chambers. Anyone attending a meeting had to check their phones, tablets, laptops, watches and fitness trackers. The last one seemed a little strange, why would a vampire be worried about staying fit?

"Then go find a TV."

"Can't leave my desk during my shift." Another rule. The vampire council loved rules.

Éduard put the phone down and said, "Sylvia doesn't believe me."

Larthia took the phone from Éduard. She put it on speakerphone. "Syl, Larthia here."

"Hey, girl."

"Just listen." Larthia held the phone toward the TV, which showed chaos and lurching dead bodies from all over the world.

"Not a g'day, mate!" an Australian announcer shouted. "They're dead and they're eatin' everyone!"

"Is that *Wyrmwood*?" Sylvia asked. "Haven't seen that."

Larthia picked up the remote and changed the channel.

23

Anderson Cooper, .45-caliber pistol in hand, reported that the CNN studios had been overrun. He fired at Christiane Amanpour as she staggered toward him. A gout of blood shot up from her head before she collapsed.

"That's New York, Syl, your home town. It's real."

"Oh my gawd. I'll call everyone on the council."

Larthia ended the call. "We should go to the council chamber."

"How do we get there?" Éduard asked. "The streets are full of biters."

"What do you mean, biters?" Lazarko looked puzzled.

"You know. Walkers. Roamers. Creepers. Rotters. All the names *The Walking Dead* uses to avoid calling them zombies."

"Deadites in *The Evil Dead*," Gary said.

"I see, but why not call zombies zombies?"

"Actually, Lazarko, the Romero movies didn't call them zombies either."

"You big ghostly expert, eh? Then why anyone call them zombies?"

"The popular will. The zeitgeist, you could call it."

"You call me bad word?"

"Just an expression." Gary shrugged his translucent shoulders.

"We were talking about how to get to the council chamber." Larthia put in. "Any ideas?"

"I could ask Baba Yaga for help," Lazarko said.

"The Russian witch who lives in a hut with chicken legs? You know her?" Éduard asked.

"Sure. She's a development exec at Disney."

CHAPTER FOUR

"WHAT'S A WUBER?" ÉDUARD LOOKED OVER THE DARK city from the balcony of the condo. Lights had gone out in some parts of the LA valley and fires could be seen consuming whole neighborhoods.

"Baba Yaga couldn't come herself, so she send a Wuber," Lazarko said, leaning over the railing and staring at nothing.

"Yes, but what is a Wuber?"

"Witch Uber. Broom-sharing service. Usually for witches only, but Baba say we can use in emergency."

"I see it," Larthia said. She pointed to the east.

A woman approached, sitting on a stick. No, Éduard saw a bundle of hay tied at one end. A broom. The handle was longer than normal.

"You called Wuber?" the woman asked as she got close enough. She stopped next to the balcony. She was a woman of generous proportions, wearing a robe and a pointy hat. "I'm Mary. I'll be your driver."

"You have to be kidding." Éduard looked at the skinny wooden handle. "We'll fall off of that."

Larthia put a cool hand on Éduard's shoulder. "It's magic, dear. She doesn't fall off."

"Get on or don't," the broom driver said. "We're busy tonight. The surge pricing is crazy, I'll make a fortune. I'll find other customers if you chicken out."

"I go." Lazarko was over the railing and settling on the rear of the broom handle in a few seconds.

"Come on." Larthia urged Éduard up, and using their vampire lifting power they sailed over the railing without touching it. Éduard sat on the handle behind the witch, expecting the skinny pole to dig into his rear end. Strangely, it was quite comfortable. Larthia put her arms around him.

"What about you, Casper?" the witch asked.

"Ha and ha," Gary sniffed. "I'll float along."

"I hope you can keep up." The witch made the broom move, and it really moved. In a moment the vampires and werewolf and witch were zooming over the city.

"I've never seen a broom with such a long handle," Éduard said.

"This is a limo-broom. Holds up to six, plus the driver."

"You know where we're going?" He wondered if witch blood would taste good. The smell of the witch was like dry wood and dead leaves. Nothing there to sustain him. Éduard rubbed the wound on his hand again.

"Got a personal call from Baba Yaga herself. She told me everything. We don't usually pick up anyone but witches."

"Don't witches have their own brooms?"

"Sometimes the broom is in the shop. Or they don't want to pay for parking. Or they're sick and can't drive. Lots of reasons to use Wuber."

"Does it pay well?"

"It's okay. They're going to use self-driving brooms in a few years, then what? I'll be looking for a job."

The broom sped toward Hollywood. Éduard looked down and saw people, or zombies, or both, on the streets. There were also crashed cars and a fire engine lying on its side. "I don't know how many jobs there will be after this."

"This?" the witch asked. "Oh, you mean the zombies. Things'll get back to normal. I have a pitch meeting next week, I hope things are okay by then."

"You're a screenwriter?"

"Yeah. I sold one script back in the '90's. It was the story of me and my sisters. Disney changed everything. Made it a comedy. It was terrible."

"What was it called?"

"*Hocus Pocus.*"

"That's considered a Halloween classic these days."

"The real story is much better. Now that I did this favor for Baba Yaga, maybe she'll greenlight a remake, done right. Here we go." The broom descended toward the Hollywood hills. Éduard saw the looming letters of the iconic sign appear out of the dark. The sign was not lit at night, due to the objections of the neighbors.

Landing behind the H, the broom stopped to let everyone off. Éduard stepped onto a steep hill, littered with rocks.

"That wasn't bad at all," Larthia said as she stood next to Éduard.

"Thanks to you for ride, Mary." Lazarko put his expensive shoes on the sandy soil. "This is where wampire council is?"

"Look out!" a female voice shouted from nearby. Éduard and the others saw a man in hiking clothing and boots, with a pack on his back, lurching toward them. A large piece of his left cheek was missing, showing bloody teeth. He reached for Larthia, then paused and looked confused.

"For a zombie, you're a beaut," Mary the witch shouted, pointing a short stick at the man, "but now I think that you're a newt!"

The man disappeared, and something small fell to the ground. "He can still bite, folks, so watch where you step. He's a zombie newt."

"Thanks for everything, Mary," Éduard said. "I would tip you, but I don't carry cash."

"Just talk to Baba Yaga about doing that remake." Mary waved and took off, the broom dwindling into the sky.

"Who warned us about the zombie?" Larthia asked.

"I don't know." Éduard looked around but didn't see anyone.

Just then, Gary arrived. "Whew, that witch flies fast. So this is where the vampire council meets?"

"Gary," the female voice said, much softer this time.

Gary looked at the base of the enormous H, near the service ladder. "Peg?"

The outline of a woman formed, then turned semi-solid. She was blonde, and wore old-fashioned clothes, like someone in a period piece movie. "Gary, what's going on?"

"These are my friends, Peg." Gary introduced everyone. "And this is Peg Entwhistle."

"Of course, my dear, I've heard of you." Larthia said. "You're quite famous."

"Who is she?" Lazarko asked.

"Peg jumped from the top of the H in 1932."

"What's going on?" Peg asked. "That man attacked a teenager – young people often come up here late at night – and I thought the girl was dead. But a little later she got up and walked away. Her face had been eaten off."

"Zombies, Peg. For real."

"Zombies? As in *White Zombie*?"

"No, well, sort of. Modern zombies eat people."

"I haven't seen a movie since I died."

"Just as well, I don't think you'd like modern zombies."

"We'd better go in now," Éduard said.

"Thanks, Peg. See you later," Gary said.

"Come visit more often, Gary."

The party turned to Éduard, who stood facing the steep hill behind the sign. He made an arcane symbol with his hands and muttered in a language that was forgotten before humans learned to lie to each other about how good the sex was last night.

"I think ghost lady like you," Lazarko said.

Gary looked back to make sure Peg was gone. "I've never had the heart to tell her I'm gay."

In response to Éduard's words, the hillside opened up, an entry appearing in the rock and dirt. Loose soil fell as it did, and a cloud of dust filled the air. His heightened vampire eyesight allowed Éduard to see a stone staircase leading down into the darkness. He stepped through the hole.

"We go down there?" Lazarko asked. "It smells like death."

"Death actually smells pretty good these days," Larthia said. "I gave him some expensive cologne for Christmas last year."

"Then this smells like Death did before your generous gift." Lazarko gestured. "After you."

Larthia entered the opening, followed by Lazarko and Gary. The ground closed up behind them, leaving the party in stygian darkness, except that the vampires and the werewolf all had excellent eyesight in the dark. Gary not so much, but he followed the sounds of the others, occasionally going through a section of wall but not noticing.

An ancient door blocked the way at the base of the stairs. Next to the door was a wooden box with a cover. "This is where we put our phones," Éduard said. He and Larthia put theirs in the box. Lazarko frowned but produced a large phone in a case adorned in gold and diamonds, or at least what looked like gold and diamonds.

Runes covered the door. Éduard raised his hand and said "E jalabur frontonium excabular."

Nothing happened. Éduard repeated the phrase. "Maybe they changed the password," he said.

"Speak friend and enter," Gary said.

"It's not that simple." Éduard ran his hands over the runes.

"What is speak friend and enter?" Lazarko growled.

"*Lord of the Rings*? The entrance to the mines of Moria?"

Lazarko snorted. "I am grown man, do not watch kiddie shows."

"Come to think of it," the ghost mused, "*The Return of the King* is a zombie story."

"No, it's not."

"Sure it is, Ed. The army of the dead? All those dead soldiers?"

"Ok, but they don't eat people."

"They kill people. Close enough."

"I think you conjugated the verb jalabat incorrectly," Larthia said. "Usually you are alone but this time you want a group to enter."

"Of course, how stupid of me. You are so smart. E jala-booya frontonium excabular."

A low grinding noise filled the air, and the door jerked open, just a bit, allowing fresher air into the stairwell. Éduard pushed it open further.

"Now, *Game of Thrones* is a zombie story," Gary said.

"Oh, totally." Éduard passed through the portal, followed by the rest of his party.

They entered a small, tastefully decorated cave. Paintings with cheerful scenes of vampires biting the necks of humans hung on the walls. An old fashioned red couch was next to one wall, and a polished mahogany desk sat near a large wooden door.

"Larthia! Thank gawd you're here!" Sylvia said from her seat behind the desk. She was a small middle-aged woman with black hair, wearing a business-casual blouse and skirt. Her reading glasses hung from a chain around her neck. She stood, hugging the Etruscan vampire. "It's crazy, I've been calling everybody. They're all coming."

Larthia turned to her companions. "Syl, you know Éduard of course. This is Lazarko the werewolf, and Gary the Gay Ghost."

"You brought non-vampires down here? I don't know what the council will say about that."

"We're trying to save the world, Sylvia," Éduard said. "I think we can bend a few rules."

"You know they don't like change." Sylvia gestured at the phone on the desk, a chunky black rotary phone. "They're still renting that from Ma Bell, I don't even know who they pay any more."

The air in the room stirred as the door to the stairwell opened. In strode an imposing figure in formal clothing, a white shirt and bow tie and a black cape with the collar stiff behind his neck. His thick, dark hair was slicked back. "Good even-ing," he said in a thick accent.

"Is that – " Gary said.

"Count Dracula, at your service," the man said.

"He's, I mean, you're real?"

"This is LA," Éduard said. "Our council reflects the most

common types of vampires from movies and television. Yes, this is the real Dracula."

Before the door closed another tall figure entered. Encased in a black coat with two rows of buttons down the front, he walked slowly toward the others. He was bald, with large pointed ears and two prominent front teeth. His hands were large, with very long nails.

"Count Orlok, from *Nosferatu*." Éduard said. The man bowed slightly but remained silent.

Lazarko backed away. "Is very creepy, this one."

"He's all right when he's fed recently." He glanced at the second Count. "I hope he has."

The door opened again and everyone looked toward it. They saw no one until they looked down. This figure was short, with the same kind of outfit as Dracula, a long, pointed nose and ears, and a shock of beard on his chin. He was also purple. He looked up and pointed.

"Vun, vun count. Two, two counts." He pointed at himself. "Three, three counts. Three counts. Ah ah ah ah."

Thunder rolled and lightning flashed, deep underground in the antechamber to the vampire council meeting hall.

CHAPTER FIVE

"WHAT, NO COUNT CHOCULA?" GARY ASKED AFTER THE three counts went through the door to the council chamber.

"Don't be silly. He never leaves General Mills corporate headquarters."

The outer door opened again. The next arrival was a young man with longish hair and a black t-shirt under a leather jacket.

"*The Lost Boys*," Gary stuttered.

"This is David, a biker vampire," Éduard said.

"I was so in love with you when I was a teenager. And alive."

David just gave a look of ultimate coolness and went through to the council chamber.

Right behind him came another hunk of vampire, with chiseled good looks and a serious look on his face.

"Michael here represents all the hot young male vampires on shows such as *The Vampire Diaries* and *The Originals.*"

Gary's mouth fell open and ghost drool appeared on his

lips. Michael gave him a sultry look and went toward the council chamber.

"Do you have hot young girl vampires?" Lazarko asked.

"Sure," Éduard said. "Let's see who comes in next."

As if in answer to Lazarko's question, a woman came in, wearing a low cut, tight black dress. "Maila represents Vampira and spinoffs such as Elvira," Éduard said.

"That slut stole my act!" Maila said. She proceeded to the council meeting.

"Is Elvira a vampire?" Gary asked.

"No one knows, but we're scared to ask her. And last but not least..." Éduard looked to the door as it opened once more. "The hot young female vampire from the TV shows."

The woman who came in was blonde and wore a dress that was very short, showing her legs almost all the way up. Right behind her was another vampire that Éduard didn't recognize. "And this is?" he asked.

"This is William, my cousin, he's visiting LA," the hot young TV vampire said. "He lives up in Washington State." The young man was good looking, you could even say beautiful. He seemed to have been ripped from the pages of a fashion magazine. He wore a jean jacket over a t-shirt and very tight pants.

"Wow," Larthia said.

Gary looked like he had been hit with a tire iron.

William smoldered his way into the council chamber, followed by his hot young female cousin. When he was gone, Gary burst out with, "I'm in love."

"I'd better go into the meeting," Éduard said. "When I'm here, I represent the Anne Rice type vampire. Tonight I'm even dressed for the part."

Larthia, Gary and Lazarko followed Éduard, but Sylvia held up her hand and said, "Vampires only in the chamber."

"That's not fair," Gary pouted.

"Don't tell me, I can't go in there either."

"Why not?" the werewolf asked.

"I'm a ghoul."

"You eat dead people?" Gary said. "May I say, eeeew."

"I'm like the servant in the Comte de Saint-Germain novels. Like him, I mostly eat raw chicken."

"Still eeeew."

"Who is this Saint-German?"

"A vampire, in a series of books by Chelsea Quinn Yarbro," Éduard said.

"All right, I will wait." Lazarko looked around. "Where can I sit?"

"Show them the break room, Sylvia," Éduard said. "We have to go into the meeting."

Sylvia walked to one wall and pressed a small stone, which slid inward. A door opened. "Fridge, microwave, Nespresso."

Larthia proceeded Éduard into the council chamber. The other vampires sat at a massive old Victorian table, in high-backed chairs. The small purple Count had a special chair that boosted him up so he could see and be seen.

Dracula called the meeting to order as Éduard settled into his chair. He wished he had been allowed to visit the break room first, there might be some blood in the fridge. Thirty seconds in the microwave and he would be able to banish the hunger that gnawed at him so strongly. His hand throbbed, but he didn't dare rub it, he didn't want anyone to ask about it.

"I hope this meeting is important," Dracula said. "I was in the abbey listening to ABBA when Sylvia called." Ever since living in Carfax Abbey in London, the Count had favored old, abandoned abbeys as his residences. Where he gained a fondness for the Swedish pop group, Éduard never knew.

Larthia stood up. "Esteemed council, I know this is normally a quiet night for us. I am sorry to have interrupted your rest. As you know, an outbreak of zombieism has taken place all over the world, and – "

"It has?" the hot young male TV vampire said. "Like, when?"

Larthia tried to hide her surprise. "My mate and I first became aware of it several hours ago, but the news reports suggest it has been happening for longer than that."

"I don't believe anything in the lamestream media," the hot young female TV vampire said, rolling her eyes. "I get all my news on Instagram."

"Éduard fought through hordes of zombies at the West Hollywood Halloween party."

"That's right," Éduard said, standing up. "And our condo building is full of them."

"Dude," the hot young male vampire said. "I want some of your pills." A laugh went around the room.

Larthia and Éduard exchanged a look, neither believing what they heard. "May I ask the members of the council how you got here tonight?" Larthia asked. "Didn't you see what is happening in the city?"

The two hot young TV vampires said almost simultaneously, "The studio sent a car." The male added, "and some security guys. One of them carried me up the hill to the Hollywood sign. I didn't want to scuff my Yeezys."

"There was some shouting and bang noises," the hot young female vampire said. "I think. I had my headphones on. I was listening to Cardi B on Spotify."

"Anyone else?" Larthia looked at each member of the council.

David shrugged. "Rode my bike. I'm cool, no one bothered me."

"I flew here," Dracula said.

"Helicopter?" the hot young male vampire asked.

"As a bat. I was blind as one too, my echolocation didn't reveal any zombies."

"Count Orlok?"

The severe looking Count raised his hands and looked creepy, but said nothing.

"Count von Count?"

"Ten, there are ten vampires. Ah ah ah ah." Lightning flashed and thunder crashed. Eduard wished he knew how the diminutive Count did that.

How about you, Malia?" Larthia asked.

"I was brilliant in *Plan Nine from Outer Space*," Malia muttered. I should have had a career and a self-titled movie! Not her!"

"Members of this council," Larthia said loudly, clearly annoyed. "There is a worldwide plague out there. Living humans will become rare. Blood will be hard to find. We must try to do something!"

"Makes me think of the old days," Dracula said, looking wistful. "Not that many peasants in the Carpathians, let me tell you. I had to manage the livestock carefully. It would feel good to be a real hunter again, instead of ordering out whenever I'm hungry."

"Sir, with all due respect," Éduard said, "there might be NO food soon. We vampires could be in danger."

"That hardly seems likely, young vampire," Dracula said. "There are a lot of humans out there."

"Zombies eat people twenty-four hours a day," Larthia told the elder vampire. "They don't have to stay inside at night. Their number grows exponentially. Humans will be reduced to those who are fast enough or smart enough to find someplace safe they can stay. Even then they could starve or die of thirst if they can't find food and water."

"Humans are so, like, fragile," the hot young female vampire said.

"You're deep," the hot young male vampire responded.

"I don't think things are as bad as you say. Why don't you two –" Dracula waved at Éduard and Larthia. "– look around and assess the situation. Report at the regular meeting on Friday night."

"Sir, we can't do it alone."

"I'll help." It was William, the visiting vampire from Washington State. "I can go out in sunlight."

"And he sparkles," the hot young female vampire said.

"Oh, so you're a *Twilight* vampire," Éduard said.

"Yeah." William looked embarrassed. "Please, no Team Edward or Team Jacob jokes. All that happened years ago. I barely know those guys."

"I won't tell any jokes." Éduard tried not to seem as angry as he was. "The idea that emo teenagers who sparkle in sunlight are vampires is a bigger joke than I could come up with. Besides, I keep being confused for Edward in those movies. My name is Éduard, it's French."

"Dear, be nice," Larthia said. "William is the only one who said he would help. We need him."

"As long as he doesn't have a vampire baby. That was the most ridiculous –"

"Angel and Darla had a baby. You loved that show."

Éduard had trouble arguing with that. But it wasn't the same. Joss Whedon could pull off anything. Except maybe *Dollhouse*. What was the man thinking?

"If that's it, I'm hungry and I have a delicious peasant – or rather a failed actor who thinks he's at an audition –

waiting for me," Dracula said and stood up. He regally left the room, followed by most of the other vampires.

Dracula had blood on the hoof waiting for him and Éduard couldn't find any anywhere. His stomach rumbled again. This was a different feeling than normal vampire hunger. It was if his stomach wanted solid food. That was impossible.

Larthia came close and put her hand on his shoulder. "You look even paler than most vampires."

"I am so hungry."

"Poor dear. Let's check the break room."

Éduard left the council chamber and saw some of the other vampires standing together and talking. Some were gone. The door to the break room was open. Just as he entered, he heard thunder behind him.

"Ho, my friend, how was the meeting?" Lazarko sat in a chair at a cheap plastic table. Éduard headed straight for the refrigerator. He let Larthia answer the werewolf's question.

"The council wasn't very helpful, I'm afraid. William is the only one willing to help us."

"The super model? What could he do?"

Éduard pulled open the refrigerator door. Racks inside meant to hold bags of blood were empty. The only thing there was a large plastic container with a lid. Sylvia's raw chicken, he remembered. "Damn!"

Larthia came to look. "I'm sorry. We'll get you some blood. There must be living humans left, this is the second most populated city in America."

Éduard gazed at the container of chicken. Something drew his attention to it. He felt his mouth water, something he hadn't felt since he was alive. He turned to Larthia. "Darling, why don't you organize our little Scooby Club out in the entry hall? I'll be there in a minute."

Larthia looked surprised, then worried. "What's wrong?"

"Nothing, nothing. I'll be there soon."

Larthia motioned to Lazarko, who followed her out of the break room. When he was sure everyone was gone, Éduard tore the cover off the container and picked up a piece of chicken. The smell of the raw meat was intoxicating. He knew there was something wrong. He hadn't eaten food since 1813. The pain in his hand burned, as if it had something to do with this sudden craving.

He bit deep into the chicken thigh, and stripped the meat off the bone. Then he ravenously tore into the other pieces, throwing the bones over his shoulder when he was done with them. The meat was cold and slimy, repellant to his vampire senses but satisfying to this new hunger. He found himself scraping grease off the bottom of the container and licking his fingers when all the pieces were gone.

The meat settled into his stomach, which hadn't dealt with anything other than blood for over two hundred years. The stomach trembled, unable to handle the load. It tried to heave the offending material back where it came from, but Éduard held it in with an act of will.

It was so good. It was horrible. Éduard shuddered with the sheer joy of the meal, and the repulsion that ran through him. He threw the container down, and turned, looking for more! More!

A gasp came from nearby. Looking up, the vampire saw a familiar ghostly face. Gary saw Éduard look at him and pulled back, disappearing into the wall.

CHAPTER SIX

ÉDUARD RAN TOWARD THE BREAK ROOM DOOR, SHAME and humiliation filling him. As he ducked through, he saw Sylvia coming toward him. "Sorry, sorry, sorry," he said as he rushed past, unable to look at her.

"What is going on?" he heard her yell. Éduard tried to look normal as he approached Larthia, Lazarko and Gary. Much to his disgust, William was also with them.

"Is something wrong?" Larthia asked.

"Nothing."

Gary stared at him but didn't say anything.

"I was just telling the others about the council meeting." Larthia shook her head. "Not much help."

"I guess that's it, then," Éduard said. "Nothing we can do. Might as well go home and wait it out."

Lazarko sniffed Éduard and muttered something to himself.

"The council will be expecting a report on Friday," Larthia said.

"If there's anything left to report about," Gary said.

Éduard burped loudly. Everyone stared. "Sorry. So, uh, how do we get out of here? Can you call Wuber, Laz?"

"When I get phone back."

They went through the door and closed it. Each one took his or her cell phone out of the box. On the way up the stairs, Gary said, "I wish I could use a cell phone. It would make hooking up so much easier."

"Did you ever use one?" Larthia asked. "Or did you –"

"Yup, died before they became a thing. I mean, there were big ugly ones. I wouldn't have been caught dead with one, just not the right look for me."

Gary had never spoken of how he died, at least not to Éduard. The vampire knew Gary had a partner who died in what the gay community called The Plague, but Gary never spoke about him, either.

At the top of the stairs Lazarko reached for the door handle and pulled. Weak light came in. "Great. Dawn is coming," Éduard said. "We can't go out in daylight. Now what?"

"Sir," William spoke up. "I can go out there."

"I saw the movie," Éduard snapped. "Just the first one. You couldn't pay me to sit through three more."

"The movies got a lot wrong," William said. "But I can go out in daylight."

"And sparkle."

"Yes. In strong light. Not all the time." The young vampire sounded almost ashamed.

"You sure you're a vampire? Sounds more like a fairy. You sure your name isn't Twinklebell?"

"He wants to help," Larthia said sharply. "He could just leave and make us wait for nightfall."

"I go with," Lazarko said. "I eat zombies for breakfast."

"All right."

The two vampires stood back and let Lazarko open the door. "I'll keep an eye on them," Gary said. "And report back if they get killed."

"I kill you, ghost, if you had meat on you," Lazarko growled as he went through the door. William and Gary followed.

The two vampires sat in the dark on the top step. Larthia looked troubled. "Are you going to tell me what's wrong?"

"What? Nothing." Éduard took out his phone and turned it on. It was very bright in the dark space. "You want to watch something? I downloaded *Vampire Dog* from Netflix. I don't know if it's any good, but as long as we have to wait here –"

"Vampires don't burp."

"You saw it? The dog burps?"

"You burped, my dear Éduard."

He should have known she would notice. She noticed everything. He would have blushed, if vampires blushed. "I'm sorry. It's my hand." He held out the offending body part.

Larthia took the hand and looked at it. "This should have healed long before now."

Éduard nodded miserably. "I know. But I haven't turned into one of those things, I just have these thoughts, about...eating."

"More than thoughts, from the way you smell. Lazarko smelled it too, I saw him."

"Sylvia's chicken. I ate it all. It was horrible, but I couldn't stop."

Larthia clearly felt revulsion at the thought, but controlled herself. "Are you still thirsty for blood?"

"Yes. Well, not as much. Maybe the chicken blood helped a little."

"You need some human blood and a long rest. I'm sure you will heal."

"You could take me to the doctor. There's a South Korean TV show called *Blood*, about a vampire doctor. I haven't seen it yet."

"Please stop the movie and TV references. I'm worried about you. With this zombie thing, who knows when you'll get proper rest."

"I know something we can do here in the dark while we wait."

"You do?" Larthia's voice turned soft and sultry. "What do you have in mind?"

"I also have *The Vampire's Coffin* on my phone. 1958, black and white..."

"Of course you do. All right." She settled down with her head against Éduard's chest. "Hit play." It wasn't long before Larthia relaxed, all movement coming to a halt, until she seemed to be a corpse. Her chest was still, with no breath going in an out. Not the slightest twitch of her muscles or snore betrayed her undead nature.

Éduard kept watching the bad 1958 movie. He didn't want to succumb to the sleep of the undead, this dark stairway was not a secure enough location. Only those who knew the proper incantation could open the door, but still he wanted to be sure he could react if something happened. He also wanted to hear if Lazarko or young William knocked on the door from outside.

Dracula was probably in his coffin by now, and Orlok in his. Those old-school vampires did things the traditional way. The new vamps, like the TV kids, didn't seem to sleep at all, except with each other. William was traipsing around in broad daylight. Éduard and Larthia usually slept the sleep of the dead during the day, though at home they had an antique queen-sized bed, carved with scenes straight out of Hieronymus Bosch, in which to do it. However, they could choose to be active if they so wanted.

So why the differences? Wasn't a vampire a vampire? Éduard often wondered about these things. As he wondered, he felt sleep creeping up on him like an unexpected tax audit. The bad movie limped on and Éduard's eyes closed, his phone fell into his lap, and he joined his lover in corpse-like slumber.

"Wake up!" someone shouted loudly. Éduard sprang up, vampire senses tingling, ready for anything. He was in a dark space with light on three sides. His feet skidded in sand and he almost tripped on a rock.

"Wha – who – how – " He was used to much more gentle awakenings.

"Is me," a Russian-accented voice said.

Éduard had trouble getting his bearings. He was safely shielded from the sun by a roof over his head, but there were no walls. He shaded his eyes from bright sunlight, and saw wild plants. He felt uneven, as if he would fall if he stepped incorrectly. He realized the ground he stood on sloped steeply downwards.

"It's all right," Larthia said. She put her hand on his arm. "We're safe, for now."

"Where are we?"

"We found friends," Lazarko said. He gestured uphill, toward the only side of the roof that did not show bright light. Éduard realized he was on a hillside, and the ground rose to meet the roof. Standing there were two very large people.

"Um, hello."

The two were ugly and hairy, with arms long enough to reach their knees. They had large, knobby noses. They were taller than Peter Mayhew, who played Chewbacca in *Star Wars*, or Ted Cassidy, the original Lurch on *The Addams Family*. They both smiled in a frightening way and cheerfully said, "Hello!"

"Hello," Éduard said, trying to be polite rather than run away screaming. "I'm Éduard Forrier."

"We know," one of the large figures said. "Larthia told us."

"They're trolls, dear," Larthia said. "Peter and Donna."

That was a bit of a shock. Éduard had assumed that trolls were from the realm of fairy tales. And that they had names like "Aaargh" or "Killyou."

"And here I thought trolls lived under bridges."

"It's sort of a bridge," Peter said in a voice like rocks grinding. At least Éduard thought the one on the left was Peter. They didn't wear clothing, but both had hair that covered their private areas. The one on the right had hair covering her chest also.

"Is Hollywood Hills house, on stilts. See?" Lazarko pointed out the steel and cement columns that held up the roof. Or rather, the house. Looking up, Éduard saw what was clearly the underside of a house, with steel beams keeping it solid, at least until the next earthquake.

"How did we get here?" Éduard asked. "I assume our new friends can't go out in sunlight either."

Donna answered, in a voice like somewhat finer rocks grinding, "It is true, we would turn to stone."

"I bring. Wrapped you in blankets. Sparkly guy killed zombies that got in way." Lazarko saw a bloodstain on his jacket. "Must take suit to dry cleaner, if there are any left."

Éduard looked at Larthia. "Did you know about this?"

"Only afterward. They woke me up here, just before you."

"How did you get in the door? Only council members know the secret incantation."

"Gary remember what you say before. Good memory, for ghost."

"I guess that answers all my questions. Oh, where did you get blankets?"

Lazarko pointed up. "Peter and Donna broke into house. People not there."

"We were hungry," Donna said. "We usually eat rabbits, deer, coyotes..."

"And sometimes a homeless person who wanders down here," Peter added.

"But the zombies made us afraid to go far. So we looked for food in the house."

"Why don't you eat the zombies?"

Peter made a face. "Smell bad."

Éduard could agree with that. His own hunger was returning, and there was nothing appetizing around him. The trolls smelled dusty, like ancient magic. He didn't want to know what their blood would do to him.

"If food is in house, I want to go." Lazarko started walking toward where the house met the hill. The trolls followed him, so Éduard shrugged and did the same. Larthia walked by his side.

"Where are Gary and William?" Éduard asked Larthia.

"Out scouting around."

Peter reached up to the floor of the house when it was close enough and his hand disappeared into a hole. He grabbed something and pulled himself up. His body and finally his feet entered the house. Then his hands came down. Donna took them and she was pulled up.

Everyone in turn was hauled into the house. The hole in the floor was rough, clearly punched through by the trolls.

Inside, Éduard saw a simple two bedroom, one-level house, that no doubt cost over a couple of million dollars. The shades were all drawn, so there was enough light to see but no one was going to burn up or turn to stone.

"What food is there?" Lazarko asked, heading for the kitchen.

"We ate some beef that was there," Donna said.

"And some smoked sausage," Peter added.

"Oh, and a little dog that was running around."

"How are you doing, Éduard?" Larthia asked.

"I need blood soon. Very soon."

"I too feel the need."

Lazarko opened the refrigerator. "There isn't much." He pulled out a plastic container with a lid and looked inside. "Quinoa. Bleh."

"Hey everyone." Gary arrived through the wall. "Glad you made it safely," he said to the vampires.

Using his supernatural strength, William jumped up through the hole in the floor and stood in the living room. "Hi. Not good out there. Zombies everywhere."

"William is a natural zombie killer. He can take the top of a head off with one blow."

"I had a blast. I never knew how fun it was to tear human beings apart."

"Here's something," Lazarko said, turning from the refrigerator with another container in his hand. "Oh, hi Gary, glitter guy. Didn't see you come in." He took off the top of the container. "Oooh, homemade chocolate chip cookies."

Gary uttered a short laugh. "I could say something, but –"

"But what?" Lazarko said through a mouthful of cookies.

"You wouldn't like it."

"Is pun, isn't it?"

Gary nodded. "I so want to say it."

"Just get it over with, Gary," Éduard said.

Gary looked at the container in Lazarko's hands, then at Peter and Donna, then at the structure around them.

"Trollhouse cookies."

CHAPTER SEVEN

THE FEMALE ZOMBIE WORE AN EXPENSIVE TAILORED suit, with a hairstyle that must have cost hundreds of dollars every time she visited her stylist. She had perfect makeup, a necklace and earrings from Bulgari, and a gaping hole in her cheek that revealed her upper and lower teeth clacking together as she attacked. Éduard waited for her to get close enough, then drove a tire iron through her botoxed forehead. She fell to the ground.

The zombies didn't want to eat the vampires, once they got a whiff of the undead scent of them, but they came close enough that there was a risk of more bites before they realized their mistake. Éduard didn't want to take that risk, his one wound still throbbing and unhealed.

They also might mob any individual and bury him or her under a pile of gnashing corpses, which didn't sound pleasant in the least.

The unlikely party that consisted of two vampires, a werewolf, a ghost, and two trolls (All right, three vampires, Éduard thought, if you counted William.) had waited until nightfall before venturing onto the narrow, winding streets of the Hollywood Hills to continue their quest. In this neighborhood the zombies were rich, though not all were as well dressed as the woman who Éduard had just skewered. Some of them had made the choice to dress like slobs just to prove how rich they were.

The streets were so narrow that in some places two cars couldn't pass each other. The houses on one side sat on the side of the mountain, and those on the other were built on the steep slope downward or were on stilts such as the adopted home of Peter and Donna.

"Most stilt houses have trolls," Donna had said when asked. "But they stay close to home." She didn't think any of the others could be recruited to the cause.

Having decided to help, the troll couple proved to be excellent zombie slayers. The stumbling dead didn't notice them at all, allowing the trolls to get close and crush their heads with one hand. Lazarko attacked in wolf form, Larthia proved handy with a butcher knife taken from the stilt house, and Gary was scout, making sure there were no surprises around the next curve of the street.

The plan was to find a large SUV with four-wheel drive, and cruise over piles of bodies or anything else that got in the way. That type of vehicle was common, but the streets were often blocked by crashed cars, and in one case a fire truck that had arrived too late to save either the burning house or the fire fighters. Several zombies in firefighting gear roamed the area. Éduard and his friends dispatched them without too much trouble.

"That one looks perfect," Larthia said. A Jeep Grand Cherokee was stalled in the middle of an intersection. One street led down the steep hill, the others went up in three directions.

"Looks clear down to Los Feliz," Gary said.

Éduard peered through the driver's side window. "We would need keys to unlock and start it."

"Maybe in one of the houses," William suggested.

"Which one?" Éduard asked. Then he gave a start as something moved inside the vehicle. It was a man, who sat up and stared with wide eyes. "People?" he said. "You talk? You're alive?"

"Well," Éduard started, but Larthia spoke up. "Is this your Jeep?"

"Thank god, thank you, thank you." The man opened the driver's side door. "I've been trapped in there all day." He stepped down onto the street. "Where are you going? Is there someplace safe?"

Éduard walked around the car. He noticed the troll couple standing down the street, not wanting to be seen by a living man. Lazarko had resumed his human form.

"We were hoping to find a sturdy vehicle, such as yours," Larthia said. "Do you have the keys?"

"I'm out of gas. I stopped and then those things covered the car, moaning and trying to get to me. It was horrible. They finally gave up and went away. I'm Joe, Joe Hannergan."

"You're fine now, Joe." She leaned in and sniffed the man. "Very fine."

Éduard could smell something good too. Beside the stench of urine. Joe must not have had a choice when stuck in his car for so long. The good smell was blood; deep, rich, fulfilling blood.

"I'm so glad you found me. I would have been eaten."

"We wouldn't want that," Larthia whispered. Then she struck, sinking her fangs into the mans' neck. Éduard raced up to her and did the same to Joe's wrist, where an artery provided a river of crimson glory.

In a few moments, Joe slumped to the ground. Éduard felt wonderful, he finally had the sustenance that his body demanded. He looked at Larthia, she had the glow of the recently sated.

"Why did you do that?" William asked. "You didn't leave any for me."

"Sorry," Éduard said. "There might be a little."

William took his turn and within thirty seconds had drained the last of Joe's blood. "While you're there," Larthia told him, "find his keys."

"Got 'em." William dangled the keys from one hand.

"We'll take the meat," Peter the troll said as he came close to the Jeep. He hoisted Joe's body over one shoulder. "I think we'll head home. You folks should be okay from here."

"I have a good recipe for human," Donna said, smiling.

"Don't trolls eat their meat raw?" Larthia asked.

"That's the recipe. So long." The trolls started back up the street toward their sort-of bridge.

Éduard felt a strange roiling in his stomach. He tried not to let it show on his face. The human blood, plus raw chicken, might not be a good combination. His hand hurt more than ever.

William insisted on driving. "We have all kinds of twisty roads up in Washington. And lots of rain. I bet I'm the best driver here."

Éduard almost said, "That's fine, since we know you're the worst vampire here." But that really was fine with him, he had never been comfortable driving cars. A good horse and carriage was how people should get around.

"I've been checking what's ahead," Gary said, appearing

out of nowhere, "I hope this heap has some serious four-wheel drive."

"I call shotgun!" Lazarko shouted, getting in the front passenger seat. Éduard and Larthia sat in the back. As they drove down the steep street, Larthia said, "Dear, you haven't mentioned a movie title since we met the trolls."

"I asked Peter and Donna what movies they like. They've never seen one! I told them since they have a house now, they should try it. I suggested the Norwegian flick *Troll Hunter*, the animated Netflix show *Trollhunters*, the campy classic *Troll 2*..."

"And the animated movie *Trolls*?"

Éduard shook his head. "Just the trailer for that made me feel ill." Just like I feel now, he thought.

Gary poked his head through a window and said, "I'll scout for you."

"Why don't you sit in the car?"

Gary smiled at Larthia. "If I sit in the car, when the car moves it will leave me behind. I go through everything."

Éduard thought about that for a second. "Can't you make yourself move forward with the car?"

"I have to match the exact speed, and all the turns. It's just easier to float outside. Besides, I can spot zombies from above and warn you."

"Good man. Er, ghost."

Gary saluted and pulled his head out of the car.

The jeep got them to the bottom of the hill, where they could turn on the much larger street Los Feliz. "Where to?" William asked.

"We go my place."

"You sure, Lazarko?" Éduard asked. "Our condo isn't too far."

"My place is closer. My wife probably worried about me."

William put his hands on the wheel. "You're my GPS, Mr. Lazarko."

"No gee pee ezz. I tell you."

"That's what I meant."

"Do I look like Siri?"

"No, I mean, you're..."

"I would like to meet that Siri."

"What?"

"She sounds sexy."

William turned his head to look at the werewolf. "Seriously."

"Not Seriously. Siri. I bet she have dark hair and legs that never end."

"She's a computer voice."

"With dark hair and legs that never end. Let me have fantasy."

"Oooookay. Which way?"

"Right."

William turned the SUV toward West Hollywood. The city was in chaos. Bodies littered the streets, glass from store fronts lay in shards everywhere. A BMW and a Hummer had crashed and burned, leaving nothing but twisted metal hulks.

William zigged and zagged through the streets, avoiding zombies if possible, hitting them hard if not. Blood and splinters of skulls soon adorned the hood of the jeep. A shabbily dressed zombie wearing a cardboard sign that read HOMELESS PLEASE HELP GOD BLESS hit just right so that he rolled into the windshield, severely cracking it, then up onto the roof, where he stayed, still moaning.

"Car's taking a beating," William said. "Won't last much longer."

"Don't worry, have plan." Lazarko grinned.

Choosing the path of least resistance, the vampires and werewolf found themselves approaching the intersection of Hollywood and Highland. Once run down and dirty, the revitalized area now featured a three-story mall, a movie theater complex, and the large theater that hosted the Oscar ceremony every year and was named after whichever corporation had most recently ponied up a few million dollars.

Across the street was the El Capitan theater, used as a showcase for Disney's most recent product, and next to the mall was the legendary Chinese Theater, with the hand and footprints of movie stars from the silent era onward in the cement in front of the theater.

"Don't go that way," Gary said, poking his head through both the roof and the homeless zombie. William slowed down as he saw an army of tourists, many of them from Japan, Korea, and other Asian countries, blocking the street. They staggered and moaned in typical zombie fashion.

William did a U turn and the inhabitants of the car found themselves facing Superman, Batman, Sponge Bob, Captain Jack Sparrow, and other movie characters, and someone dressed as a movie zombie, who was now really a zombie.

"Who are they?" William asked.

"Unemployed actors, mostly," Éduard said. "They walk around here hoping to get tips from tourists who take their pictures."

Frankenstein's monster, apparently carrying a cage in which a black man was confined, walked in front of the jeep. "That's clever," Larthia remarked. She was right, the illusion that the monster was carrying the man was well done, the man using his own legs inside the monster's pants while the head and arms of the creature were fake. The illusion worked less well because the man was slumped over in the cage, working his jaw in a chewing motion, his left hand and forearm missing, and the whole contraption barely staying upright as he stumbled over big monster boots.

William gunned the engine and sped toward the thinnest line of zombie characters. The jeep plowed into Wonder Woman and Spider-Man with a crunch. Blood sprayed the windshield. Behind them were a cluster of tourists, carrying bags from the many souvenir shops that lined Hollywood Boulevard. They provided more of a barrier, the SUV grinding to a halt as their various body parts, LA sweatshirts with pictures of the beach on them and fake Oscar statuettes were caught in the wheels.

"Go!" Éduard said as the car made strange noises in response to William's attempts to start it.

"I can't!"

Lazarko opened his door and got out. "Can't live forever!" he shouted and plunged into the crowd in wolf form, tearing zombies apart.

Larthia opened her door too. "We can't let him fight alone."

"What?" Éduard said. "We'll never make it through that."

"Lazarko is the only one of us who is alive, and he's risking his neck."

Eduard lowered his voice. "I don't want more bites." He definitely didn't want more of the strange effect of the bite, which he could still feel even though he had fed.

"I'm going." Larthia slipped out of the Jeep.

"Wait!" Éduard stepped on the street on his side. "Come on, Bill, you're dead too." He turned and grabbed a plump woman with a selfie stick in her hand. She looked surprised when he put his hand in her mouth and ripped the top of her skull off, exposing her brain. Éduard was a little surprised by this too, especially since it didn't stop her. Eyeless and with no head to speak of, the woman still walked. The vampire took the selfie stick from her and beat the brain to a pulp. This finally dropped her.

"Don't call me Bill," William said, coming up behind Éduard. He sounded angry. Obviously Éduard had hit upon a sore spot. Despite that, he took out a man, woman and eight-year-old boy who no doubt were on a family vacation they had dreamed of for years, simply by punching each one in the nose, his hand disappearing into each ruined face.

"And I'm not dead, exactly."

"Is that right?" Éduard asked.

Larthia reached into the cage that Frankenstein's Monster held and put the poor man out of his misery with her knife. The man, cage, and fake monster fell to the street.

"My heart doesn't beat, or blood flow," William said, "but I have a soul. I think I do. Other members of my community believe we are soulless."

"How nice." Éduard picked up a zombie with gnashing teeth and threw it over some others. He knew it would be back, but he was being pressed on all sides and had little time to deal with each one. "If sunlight doesn't kill you, what about wooden stakes? Garlic? Silver?"

William shook his head, dismantling a city bus driver and tossing her pieces back into the crowd. "Nothing really."

"Come on, there's always something, or you have a bad story."

"Well, cutting us up and burning us is about it. We're super strong and bullets bounce off us."

Éduard plunged his fingers into the eye sockets of a Japanese man with two cameras hanging from his neck. The man went slack and fell. "Just as I thought, bad story."

"What?" William said, over the moaning and the noise of slaughter.

"Nothing."

CHAPTER EIGHT

F OR EVERY ZOMBIE THAT ÉDUARD PUT DOWN, SEVERAL more took its place. He tried to stay close to Lazarko, the only living member of the group and therefore the center of the zombie attack. The Russian werewolf tore off heads and severed limbs left and right. Larthia and William held their own, but it was clear that overwhelming numbers would prevail before too much longer.

Concentrating on destroying zombies, Éduard at first didn't notice the sound of a drum. He did notice the sound of Gary's voice. "You have to see this," the ghost said, close to the vampire's ear.

"Busy, Gary."

"You're getting help."

When he had a second to turn his head, Éduard saw a man in Chinese robes, beating on a drum. More men, a lot of them, also in robes and Chinese hats, came toward the cluster of zombies and zombie fighters. Éduard was astonished to see that they held their arms straight in front of them, and instead of walking or running, they hopped.

The hopping matched the rhythm of the drum. As the

strange men got close to a zombie, they picked it up and threw it, or tore at its neck with very long fingernails. Heads fell back, attached to bodies only by the spine. These zombies wandered around, only able to see behind them.

"Jiang Shi," Éduard said.

"What?" Gary asked.

"Chinese vampires, or zombies. Undead, anyway. What are they doing here?"

The new fighters, strange as they were, were effective enough that the ranks of the zombies thinned out somewhat. Larthia dispatched a tall tourist with one thrust of her knife into his nasal cavities, then turned to see the Jiang Shi.

"Aren't they from that Hong Kong movie you watched?"

"They're in a lot of Asian movies." Éduard crushed the head of a short woman, who collapsed to the pavement. "They're very popular over there."

The zombie horde was reduced enough that the fighters could stop and assess the situation. The man with the drum approached them, still pounding out the rhythm. The hopping vampires formed a circle around everyone, keeping zombies out.

"Thank you for your help, sir." Eduard addressed the man.

The man bowed. "I am Wu Keung, necromancer and film distributor. I study the black arts and import Asian films to America."

"You control these things?" Lazarko asked.

"Indeed. As long as I beat the drum I am their master."

"In the movies, they suck life force – qi – from people," Éduard said. "The zombies are dead and have no qi."

"It is so. However, the Jiang Shi follow my commands, and I decided to help when I saw your group. You are vampires?"

"Three of us are. I'm Éduard, this is Larthia and William. Lazarko is a werewolf and Gary is a ghost."

"Most unusual group to be fighting zombies."

"Larthia thought maybe we could find a way to end the zombie apocalypse."

Wu Keung raised his eyebrows. "I do not know how to accomplish such a goal, but I wish you well. I live nearby, I can offer you a safe place to stay for a while."

"We were going to Lazarko's place in West Hollywood. Can you help us get there?"

"I think you should not be in the open much longer." Wu Keung gestured toward the east, where a sliver of sun showed over the dinosaur attacking a clock above the Believe It or Not Museum.

"Already? Larthia, we need to hole up. Mr. Wu is offering his place."

"We graciously accept, Mr. Wu," Larthia said. "The rest of you can do what you want, but we vampires – except William – need to get inside."

"I could use sleep," Lazarko, now in human form, said.

"My kind doesn't sleep," William said, "but I will stay with the group."

"You don't sleep?" Éduard said, annoyed. "Really? Do you have any weakness? Are you just super duper, beautiful and perfect?"

"Pretty much."

"Lazy writing." Éduard muttered.

"What?"

"Nothing."

Wu Keung, still beating his drum, moved the circle of Jiang Shi toward the fabled Chinese Theater. Zombies seemed to have lost interest in attacking the group, maybe the smell of the undead overwhelmed the scent of Lazarko, the one living being.

"Kinda funny, you living near the Chinese Theater." Éduard remarked to Mr. Wu.

"Not at all. I chose this area because of it. It is famous throughout the world and is both a reminder of home and related to my business."

"It's not really Chinese, it's a cheesy 1920's American vision of Chinese."

"True, but it has been converted to IMAX and has an amazing sound system and auditorium seating. I much prefer it to the multiplex theaters inside the Hollywood and Highland mall."

Still with hopping Jiang Shi around them, everyone moved up a side street, toward the Magic Castle. Wu Keung took a remote from his pocket and pressed a button. A nearby steel door in the side of a building, big enough to admit a panel truck, rattled open. The whole group entered and the door closed. A larger steel panel slid down inside and solidly thunked into a slot in the floor. No zombies would get through that.

Wu Keung rattled a different rhythm on his drum and the Jiang Shi turned as one toward the far side of the room. Éduard saw three rows of coffin-sized wooden boxes near the far wall. Each of the hopping vampires settled into a box and lay still, putting its arms down so presumably a lid could be put on the box.

The room was large, the brick walls rising high enough that the seventeen-foot-tall statue of David by Michelangelo wouldn't hit his marble head on the dirty, off-white ceiling. Besides the boxes now containing Chinese vampires, many other boxes contained DVDs of Asian zombie, vampire, and every other variety of supernatural-themed movies.

"You have *Train to Busan*." Éduard picked up a selection of movies. "Best zombies on a train movie ever. And *Bio-Zombie, Wild Zero, Tokyo Zombie*...and here's one Larthia won't like."

"What?" Larthia took the DVD out of Éduard's hand. "*Big Tits Zombies*." She threw it on one of the piles. "I've told you that even horror movies should respect women." She walked away. Éduard picked it up and tucked it under his shirt. He silently mouthed "Pay you later" to Wu Keung, who nodded.

"You never watch ghost movies," Gary said, appearing at the vampire's side.

"Well, there are plenty of them from Asia. You can come to my house and watch them if you want."

"If things return to normal," the ghost muttered.

Welcome to my office, home, and headquarters," Wu Keung said. "The vampires are welcome to stay the day. I can provide a shipping box for each, just as my Shiang Ji use.

"That's fine," Larthia said.

"The werewolf may sleep, if he likes. I have no bed, I'm afraid."

"Just give me a blanket."

"The ghost may...float."

"I'll be around," Gary said.

"I don't sleep." William looked around. "Just give me a place to sit and obsess over a high school girl I met while pretending to be a teenager."

"You ARE part of that story!" Éduard exclaimed.

"Just kidding. Maybe I'll watch some of the movies."

"There is an office with a TV and player through that door." Wu Keung pointed to a small exit in the rear.

Éduard and Larthia settled into two empty boxes.

Lazarko took the blanket he was given and turned around in circles several times before lying down with a sigh. The lethargy of daytime overtook Éduard and he felt himself slip away into the dreamless sleep of the dead.

When he woke, something was wrong. His limbs would not respond to his will. He could only stare at the high ceiling. He tried to call out to Larthia but could not speak. He heard someone moving around but couldn't tell who it was. Nothing happened for what seemed a very long time, Éduard growing more and more frantic.

Finally, the figure of Wu Keung appeared above him. The necromancer smiled. "Good evening, my new slaves." He played something on his drum, something different than when he controlled the Jiang Shi. Suddenly Éduard could move, but only in limited ways. He could sit up, then climb out of the box and stand. If he thought to do anything else, his muscles didn't respond.

Larthia then did the same, standing next to her box. Her movements were jerky, without her usual grace.

"I allow you limited speech," Wu Keung said, playing a little trill on his drum. Éduard's jaw unlocked. "What are you doing?"

"Adding two American vampires to my herd, and very pleased to do so."

"I'm French," Éduard said.

"Etruscan," Larthia added.

"Western vampires, then. Distinct from my beloved, but not very bright, Jiang Shi. I can't hold a conversation with them, as I am with you."

"What are you going to do with us?"

"You are the start of my undead army. I will carve out an empire and rule with an iron fist."

Éduard tried to look around for Lazarko, or Gary. He couldn't turn his head. "You do realize that's insane."

"Insane is a little harsh. I would call it megalomaniacal."

Larthia grimaced, which must have been very hard for her. "Your drum controls zombies too?"

"Alas, no, I need a spell for that, which I don't have with me. Now, as my slaves, help me prepare for my destiny."

One jazzy drum solo later, and Éduard felt his muscles ease up. He could move, but only in response to Wu Keung's orders, who beat his drum in a way that the vampire could not resist. The work consisted mainly of nailing lids on the boxes that contained Jiang Shi. The Chinese vampires lay inert in their crates as the lids were attached. Wu Keung must be planning to ship them somewhere.

As he worked, Éduard felt hunger come over him once again. He had fed well the night before, but the lust for blood always came back. He had another hunger too, one he was ashamed to admit to himself. The raw chicken he had filled his belly with was long gone, though how was a mystery. Vampires didn't poop, and neither did zombies, at least they didn't in any movie he had seen. He had wondered where the flesh they ate went. And you never saw a zombie refuse a meal because he or she was full. They were always ready for more.

Unable to solve this question at the moment, Éduard nevertheless felt a desire for more raw chicken. Or raw something. The bite on his hand throbbed, and still was not healed. A rumbly in his tumbly told him that flesh from any creature would not be unwelcome there.

He saw no sign of Gary, Lazarko, or William. He hoped they were unhurt. Though he had disparaged William's too-easy strength and other attributes, a super-strong, diamond-hard rescuer would be welcome.

Finding himself near Larthia as he worked, Éduard managed to whisper, "Any idea how to escape?"

"I fear not. Wu Keung's power seems to control vampires absolutely."

That jogged Éduard's memory. "He said he needed a separate spell to control zombies."

"I heard that. What are you thinking?"

An idea tickled the back of Éduard's brain. An idea he didn't like, but the only idea he had. "Darling...I am going to attempt something. If it goes badly, remember that I love you."

"What are you thinking?" Larthia repeated, alarmed. Éduard moved away from her, toward the drum-beating necromancer.

"Continue your work, vampire." Wu Keung beat his drum harder. "I am your master."

Éduard concentrated on his hunger. Not his lust for the crimson liquid that sustained his vampiric existence, but the new hunger. The one that made him desire to feel flesh in his jaws, to chew, to crush human tissue to pulp, and swallow.

"What are you doing?" the necromancer shouted as Éduard advanced on him. "My drum controls vampires with power absolute!" By the time he finished that pronouncement, Éduard was no longer a vampire. His zombie hunger overwhelmed him. He reached for the nearest source of sweet, succulent meat and moaned like an extra on *The Walking Dead*.

Wu Keung threw up his arms but it was too late. Eduard forced his chomping jaw onto the necromancer's neck and sank his teeth, not just his fangs but all of his teeth, into the soft skin and took a bite. He ripped out a chunk of flesh, severing the jugular vein and causing blood to wash over his face and run down his body, creating massive stains in his Louis de Pointe du Lac costume that would never come out.

Another bite ended the life of the necromancer Wu Keung. The drumming stopped. Éduard stood over the corpse, dripping blood. Larthia rushed up to him. "You're...you're..." she stammered.

The zombie that had been elegant eighteenth-century-style-vampire Éduard Forrier turned to stare with no sign of intelligence in his eyes. He moaned once, then straightened. His eyes flickered. "Eating him, is what I think you're trying to say." He picked a gobbet of flesh out of his teeth with a long fingernail. "He could use some salt."

CHAPTER NINE

"**A**RE YOU ALL RIGHT?"

Eduard dropped the necrotic necromancer to the floor and said, "I think so. I gave into the zombie influence from my bite. He said he didn't have the proper spell for controlling zombies, so I thought maybe he couldn't control me."

"It seems to have worked, darling." Larthia stood apart from her lover, clearly not sure what to think of him at that moment. "But how did you return to your normal self?"

"I don't know. Now that flesh in my belly is beginning to make me a little queasy."

"Maybe we should give up this quest. There's nothing we can do to stop an apocalypse. We should hole up in our condo and see what happens."

Éduard looked thoughtful. "If it's all the same to you, dear, I would like to continue. I now want to find a cure for myself as much as for the world."

The conversation was interrupted by the sounds of quite a few Jiang Shi struggling in their boxes. "They are no longer under the necromancer's control," Larthia said. "They seek freedom."

"Before they find it, we should exit stage right."

"What about the others?"

Éduard looked around but so no sign of their companions. "Let's check the room where William was going to watch movies."

The door in the back took the vampires past a number of Jian Shi boxes, all of them shaking as their occupants sought a way out. "They will break out," Éduard said. "I don't know if they will attack us, but I would rather not find out."

A heavy bar kept the door well and thoroughly locked. Éduard lifted it off and turned the handle. It moved easily. He pulled the door open. Inside there was no comfortable TV room, no TV at all, and no Blu-Ray player. An industrial style window showed that night covered LA.

There were shelves along the walls of the small room. On the shelves were many jars. In one corner was a cage, and curled up inside was one Russian werewolf, in wolf form. He didn't react as the vampires approached. "Lazarko!" Éduard said loudly, trying to wake up his friend. There was no response.

The sound of glass moving on wood came from one wall. Larthia pointed upward. "That jar is shaking."

Something swirled inside the jar. Éduard reached a hand up, then jerked it back when a face resolved inside the jar. "It's Gary," Larthia said.

It was indeed. Éduard reached for the jar again and took it down. Gary's face formed again. His lips moved but no sound could be heard. With no better idea how to free the ghost, the vampire threw the jar hard onto the cement floor, where it shattered into many pieces.

"Thank you!" Gary said, inflating to his normal size. "Where is that necrofucker?"

"He's dead," Larthia said. "Éduard ate him."

"That's good. Wait, ate him?"

"It's a bit of a story," Éduard told the ghost. "Let's get out of here before I tell it to you. How do we wake up Lazarko?"

"I saw Woo Kong or whatever his name was through my jar. He slipped Lazarko a mickey in some food, then stuffed him in the cage and put some kind of spell on it."

"Let's see if vampiric strength can open it." Éduard pulled and pulled on the door of the cage, only managing to bend the metal bars, not break them. "How about double the vampiric strength?"

Larthia joined in, and after a good ten seconds of straining, the lock gave way and the door came cleanly off the cage. Inside, the werewolf snoozed on. Éduard leaned in and dragged him onto the floor.

"What? What Iz?" Lazarko rolled on his back and changed to human form, his suit and jewelry appearing from wherever they went while he was a wolf. "What happened?"

"No time, let's go," Éduard said.

"Where's William?" Larthia asked. "Lazarko, did you see what happened to him?"

The werewolf shook his head. "I eat something, I sleep."

"We don't need him anyway." Éduard spoke as if he didn't care, but he had to admit to himself that the crepuscular vampire was handy to have around.

"Wait," Gary said. "Smash all the jars."

"We don't have much time."

"Please. Kung Fu collected ghosts. I don't want to leave them like this."

Lazarko grinned. "No problem, my friend." He leaped

into action, sweeping the jars off the shelves. As each one broke into many pieces, a ghost fled, passing through the walls before any of the assembled crew saw who or what they were.

Éduard and Larthia joined the fun, destroying all the glass prisons. Soon the floor was covered in shards and the shelves were empty. One ghost emerged from the chaos, but didn't flee. It resolved into the shape of a man with dark hair and handsome features.

Gary gave a gasp as the ghost's face became clear. "Guys...do you know who this is?"

"Where am I?" the ghost asked. He looked around. "Is this a set?"

Éduard then recognized the man too. He had only seen a couple of his films, but the face was hard to forget. "Montgomery Clift?"

The ghost looked at the vampire. "Sure. Who's asking?"

"I had such a crush on you when I was in high school." Gary had a big smile on his face.

"You had a crush on me? You're a guy. I'm not like that."

"it's all right, Monty, it's the twenty first century, you don't have to hide any more. Besides, you're dead."

Monty shook his ghostly head. "I can't be dead. I'm shooting *From Here to Eternity*."

"You are ghost. Outside is a zombie apocalypse," Lazarko said. "And I like *Red River* better. Mostly because of John Wayne. You were okay."

The handsome ghost looked confused. "What do you mean zombie? I don't do B pictures. No scary stuff."

"Don't worry about it," Gary said. "You're free, zombies won't bother you."

"You people are weird. I have to get back to my room at the Roosevelt. I'm working on my lines." The ghost of Montgomery Clift floated toward the wall, then stopped in mid-air and turned around. "Where's my trumpet?" He flowed through the wall and disappeared.

"What was that about a trumpet?" Larthia asked.

"People hear him playing it in the hall of the Roosevelt Hotel, outside Room 928. He stayed there while he was filming *From Here to Eternity* in 1953."

"Montgomery Clift was gay?" Lazarko asked.

"Of course, all the best actors back then were gay."

"Like who?"

"Honey, we don't have time to list them all. What's that?" Gary pointed to one last jar on a shelf. It was smaller than the others, a mason jar with a metal lid. Éduard took it down and saw swirling colors inside. The swirls briefly formed a female figure with wings, then turned back into colors.

Éduard tried to open the lid of the jar, but his vampire strength wasn't enough. He rapped it on a wall, but it didn't break. The only thing left was to fling it hard to the floor. It thunked and rolled, undamaged. Éduard picked it up and put it in a coat pocket.

What's that noise?" Larthia asked.

The sound from the main room suggested that a lot of the Jiang Shi had escaped their boxes. "We'd better get going." Éduard walked toward the door. "Stay close, protect Lazarko."

"I have better idea." Lazarko picked up the cage and rammed it through the window. Glass and the steel frame fell outward, leaving a large opening. He looked pointedly at Gary. "Ladies first."

"You are such a wit," Gary said, not moving. He leaned forward and seemed to pick something up off the ground. He made a throwing motion and shouted, "Fetch!"

Lazarko jumped through the window, then called back. "Damn you!"

Éduard and Larthia held hands as they vampire-floated through the opening, where the night air was cool and refreshing. No zombies could be seen in the alley where they found themselves. "What now?" Éduard asked. "Find a car?"

"My place." Lazarko started trotting down the alley. "I have plenty food and many booze."

"That doesn't do us any good, we need blood." Something buzzed by Éduard's ear, making him duck a little. "What was that?"

"What was what?" Before Larthia finished the sentence she ducked too, then looked around. "Something flew by my ear."

"Bugs!" Lazarko shouted as he stopped and waved his arms around.

The air became full of flying somethings. They were bigger than bugs, several inches tall, and seem to have only four legs, plus wings.

"Give us the queen!"

Was that really a voice? Éduard thought. It was so small, so high pitched. It came again. Something landed on Éduard's ear and screeched "Give us the queen!" He tried to swat it but it was gone.

"They're going through me!" Gary said. "They have magic, I can feel it." In fact Gary's translucent form, with a street light behind him, was filled with of a swarm of the not-bugs.

They didn't have four legs, Éduard realized, they had two arms and two legs. Tiny humanoid figures with flimsy wings. They were like the figure in the jar. He took it out of his pocket and held it out. "Is this what you want?"

All of the flying things formed a cluster around the jar, so thick that Éduard could barely see his hand. "Open! Open!" the little voices chanted as one.

"I tried. It won't even break."

"Éduard?" Larthia asked, "what is going on?"

"Fairies. Their queen seems to be in the jar."

"Fairies is not real," Lazarko stated with certainty.

"Tell that to them."

"I've been called a fairy, but I never saw one before." Gary came close to the globe of flying bodies.

One little figure broke from the rest and hovered right in front of Éduard's nose. "Come with us."

"Anyone have fly swatter?" Lazarko asked. "I squish them."

The swarm flew to the werewolf and covered his head. Nothing could be seen above his neck except flapping wings. Lazarko waved his arms and staggered. After bout twenty seconds the fairies left him and he took in a huge breath. "Fairy fuckers!" He leaned over and coughed hard.

The fairy in front of Éduard repeated "Come with us."

"Let's go with them," Éduard said.

CHAPTER TEN

THE CLOUD OF FAIRIES CIRCLED THE TWO VAMPIRES, one werewolf and one ghost. As everyone moved forward, the fairies began to sing, their voices shrill. Éduard covered his ears and saw Larthia doing the same. Gary didn't seem to be bothered, but Lazarko too put his hands over his ears.

The song seemed to grab reality and shift it. The buildings in Hollywood shimmered and grew transparent. It was still night, but the quality of the light changed. The streetlights faded away but a bright moon lit the landscape. There were no cars. Grass and flowers grew over everything. A pale light, not enough to make the vampires fear bursting into flame, made everything visible.

"I wonder if Tinker Bell is one of these," Gary said as the strange new world became more solid.

"They don't seem like fairies I've seen in any movies," Larthia said.

"Don't ask me. I don't do fairy movies." Éduard looked around at their hosts and shuddered. "I tried to watch that animated George Lucas thing one night when you were out,

Larthia, but I couldn't take it. Pop songs and fantasy don't mix."

"I wonder how they taste." Lazarko swiped the air, trying to catch some, but failed.

The city didn't disappear entirely. The buildings were there, but hard to see. Wild plants grew on them. The group approached a large circle of mushrooms, where even more fairies waited, flying and talking in their high-pitched voices.

"A fairy circle," Larthia said. "Of course."

"Are they all girls?" Lazarko asked.

"I think so." Éduard tried to focus on individual fairies, but they flitted by so fast he couldn't see much detail.

"Nothing here for me then." Gary kept close to the others.

"Do you ever think of anything but sex?" Éduard asked.

"Let's see..." Gary paused for a moment. "Nope."

A fairy stopped and hovered in front of Éduard's face. He thought it was the same one as before, but he couldn't be sure. "You go in circle!" it piped.

A shiver went through him as the vampire stepped over the mushrooms. Larthia and Lazarko tried to follow, but the fairies mobbed them and pushed them back. Gary found he couldn't enter the circle, his ectoplasm flattened on an invisible barrier.

Once in the center, Éduard and the one fairy were the only beings inside the mushrooms. "Open jar!"

"I told you," Eduard said, lifting the jar in front of him again. "I can't." He saw the queen stop and look at him, then lose her coherence and swirl around inside. He put his right hand on the lid and twisted. It didn't budge. His hand still hurt a little from the zombie bite, and the strain made it hurt more.

"Humans are weak."

"Who are you calling human? I'm a vampire."

The fairy flew up close to Éduard's face. "Vampires aren't real."

"Sure we are." Éduard opened his mouth to show his fangs. He raised his hands and brandished his long, pointed nails. The fairy examined these things closely. "Vampire like in *Fright Night*?"

"You know *Fright Night*? I'm surprised fairies watch movies."

"When I was little I lived in a wooded thicket near a drive-in theater. Sometimes when my parents thought I was doing magical chores I flew up and sat on a fence and watched. My favorites were the scary ones."

"Not just movies, but horror movies. I'm beginning to like you."

The fairy looked around. "Don't tell anyone."

"Your secret is my secret. As long as you fairies help us."

"We don't help humans. Or vampires."

"I'll try to get your queen out of this jar, and you see what you can find out about how to stop the zombie apocalypse."

"Zombies like *Resident Evil*?"

"Yeah. And all its sequels."

"There are sequels?"

"Many."

"And real zombies are really real now?"

"You didn't notice?"

"I haven't been in the human world for a while. We've been so worried about the queen. Are you sure you used all your strength on that jar?"

"I did, I promise you. Could there be some magic on it?"

The fairy flew backward a bit. "Maybe. Nasty pixies put her in there. Sold her to a sorcerer."

"There you go. Pixie magic. Wait, aren't fairies and pixies the same thing?"

This enraged the fairy. "No! No!" She flew around in circles. "They are stupid, ugly. No wings!"

"Okay, okay. If pixies put her in there, maybe only they can get her out."

The fairy wasn't happy about that idea. "Pixies are bad. They will never help."

Éduard looked out past the circle of mushrooms and saw Larthia there. She seemed worried. He decided he had to try to complete their quest, so they could go back to a normal, civilized world where they could watch movies, or go for a stroll on Santa Monica Boulevard and grab an easy meal of blood from one of the many passing humans. Zombies would go back to being only on TV.

"Tell you what," Éduard said, formulating a plan as he spoke, "why don't we get everyone to help? Everyone in the supernatural community in LA. Someone out there must know how the zombie plague started and how to fix it. I will talk to the pixies about your queen too."

The fairy looked skeptical. "Fairies don't care if humans turn into zombies. Humans and all their iron and steel." She shuddered. "Poison to us."

"You live in Los Angeles. If you hate humans why not live in some forest somewhere?"

The fairy grew haughty. "I don't have to explain every-thing to a vampire. But...if it gets our queen back we will help."

"Thank you. Tell your fairies to spread the word. I want every troll, gnome, ghost, goblin, vampire, any kind of supernatural creature to know what we're trying to do."

"And what will you do?"

"Point me at the pixies."

"South."

"May I ask your name? So I can ask for you later?"

"You may ask for Beth."

"Beth?" Éduard was surprised. "I thought fairies had names like Tin –"

"Don't say it," Beth interrupted. "That's the name of a corporate cartoon. Disney doesn't own us."

"Sorry."

Beth flew away and Éduard exited the fairy circle. His friends gathered around. He explained the gist of the conversation.

"Fairies like *Resident Evil*?" Gary asked. "I would think maybe *Warm Bodies* for the romance, or maybe *Zombieland* for the comedy. And Bill Murray."

"Only Beth likes horror movies," Éduard said. "And I think you're missing the point. All the fairies are going to tell every supernatural creature in LA to help us."

"As long as we help them," Larthia said.

"Yes. So we go south."

"We were going to my house," Lazarko said.

"Change of plan, Laz."

"My wife will not be happy when I do get home."

"It's more important to meet the pixies."

"Pixy Stix?" Lazarko said. "I love that candy when I came to America as young boy."

"No, pixies. Little creatures sort of like fairies but with no wings."

"So sweet, made me feel good."

"It's just sugar in a straw," Gary said. "I'm surprised you aren't the only werewolf with diabetes."

"There will be no candy of any kind if we don't return

the world to normal," Éduard said.

Lazarko's grin faded. "I did not think of that."

"So we go south."

Gary looked around. "Which way is south?"

No one knew. They all tried to get the attention of a fairy, but they flew by so fast it was nearly impossible. Finally Larthia bellowed out "WHICH WAY IS SOUTH?"

At least dozen fairies pointed in one direction. Then one flew close. "Beth says we will allow you to stay in fairyland as you walk. Then you will safe from bomzies." She flitted away before anyone could correct her.

"South it is then." Eduard started in the indicated direction. His stomach rumbled. It had only been a few hours since he had necromancer for breakfast. He hoped something with both meat and blood would present itself along the way.

The city was still visible around them, though it seemed to be in a deep fog. Flowers and vines grew over everything. "The light never changes," Larthia noted after they had been walking for a while.

"It never gets bright enough to worry about sunlight," Éduard agreed. "And there are no cars, trucks, anything."

Gary flew off and came back a number of times. "I'd swear we just passed Staples Center," he said after one such expedition.

"That's impossible, we haven't been walking that long." Éduard turned around. He didn't see the home of the Lakers and Clippers, but the vague impressions of buildings were very tall, like the structures in the downtown area.

"I don't like," Lazarko muttered to himself over and over. "Smells wrong."

In just a few more steps, the tall buildings were gone, if they were ever there. Everything was one-story houses or two-story apartment buildings. Maybe, it was hard to tell. Everything in fairyland was vague shapes and uncertainties.

A little later the light grew brighter. Éduard felt it on his skin. Too much more and he would be fricasseed vampire. "We need to get in shade." He found the side of a wooden building and moved into the shadow next to it. As he did, fairyland went away. The city of LA crashed back into existence, bright sunlight heating the air to a sizzle. Buildings were back, and cars. Some of the cars were stalled, others crashed. One burned.

Eduard and Larthia put hands over their faces. Even looking into sunlight from shade hurt their eyes. "Where are we?" Eduard cried out.

"Is big intersection," Lazarko said. "No traffic, no people."

"Guys," Gary said. "I'm not sure you're going to believe this."

"Just tell us, Gary." Éduard said.

Moaning started nearby. People appeared and looked toward the group. They came around cars, walking slowly but surely toward the vampires, ghost and werewolf. They weren't alive.

"We're at Jefferson and San Pedro. We're in South LA."

Éduard took out his phone to Google Maps the location. Gary had to be wrong. On the main screen he saw the date. "There's something wrong with my phone."

Zombies got closer. "We can't leave the shade. Lazarko, they're after you. Find a safe place."

"I can kill a few zombies."

Many more zombies came from everywhere.

"I can kill lots of zombies."

"Um, my phone says it's November 8th. It's a week after yesterday."

CHAPTER ELEVEN

OMBIES CAME CLOSER AND CLOSER, HANDS REACHING
out, moans filling the air. Éduard saw a policeman
with one arm ending in a bloody stump above the elbow, a
grandmotherly woman with blood soaking the front of her
flower-print dress, and a young man with sagging pants and
a hole in his torso that the vampire could see through.

Lazarko launched himself into the crowd of undead in
wolf form, growling and snapping, severing limbs and
sending blood spraying. He took the fight into sunlight,
where Éduard and Larthia couldn't help him. Stumbling,
limping, and dragging dead surrounded the werewolf. He
used teeth and claws to tear into their skulls and damage
their brains. Some dropped to the ground in final death but
two or three more replaced each one.

"There must be something we can do for him," Larthia
said.

"We'll be lucky to survive ourselves." Éduard eyed the
shade, which would disappear as the sun moved.

A black Cadillac Escalade slammed into the crowd of
zombies. Some of the animated corpses were sent flying,

others were crushed under the wheels of the luxury SUV. Éduard heard a voice say something, and another reply in a Russian accent. In a moment the big car moved again, turning toward the dwindling shade where the vampires stood.

"Get in," the driver said.

With no other available options, Éduard and Larthia opened the passenger side doors of the Cadillac and sat inside. The vehicle took off as soon as they slammed the doors shut. Lazarko sat behind the driver. "See? I knew we survive."

Éduard, in the back seat with the werewolf, shook his head. "That was close. Who's driving?"

"Thank you, whoever you are," Larthia said from the front passenger seat. There was no response.

"Where's Gary?" Éduard asked.

The ghost poked his head through the window. "Sorry, I couldn't watch that. I thought you guys were goners."

"Did you see who's driving?"

Gary shook his head. "I'll follow you like before." He withdrew from the interior of the car.

"May I ask who rescued us?" Eduard asked loudly.

A deep and resonant voice filled the car. "I WAS SENT TO FIND YOU."

"Well, thank you." A low buzzing noise seemed to come from the front of the vehicle.

"Oh!" Larthia said. "There are bees in here."

It was true. Small insect bodies circled in the air, occasionally landing on the roof, the back of the seats, and Éduard's face. He waved them away.

"Let us out!" Lazarko said. "I do not like the stinging!"

"THEY DO NOT STING UNLESS I WILL IT."

The car swerved, then bumped over some obstacle, probably a zombie or two.

"I'm sorry," Éduard said, "but I really do want to know who you are and who sent you."

"YOU WILL MEET MY EMPLOYERS SOON. AS FOR ME, YOU MUST HAVE SEEN MY MOVIES."

Of course, Éduard thought. This is LA, he would have something to do with movies. "Can you describe our driver, Larthia?" he asked.

"A distinguished looking African American gentleman, in a heavy coat with fur trim. And, um, a metal hook in the place of his right hand."

"Sounds like the Candyman."

"I saw that," Lazarko commented. "Not bad."

"DO NOT SAY MY NAME."

"Surely I could say it safely, up to four times." Eduard smiled, remembering seeing the movie with Larthia in Istanbul in the early '90s. Even with his rudimentary Turkish, he understood the dubbed voices pretty well.

"NO, SAY IT NOT EVEN ONCE. I DIDN'T READ THE CONTRACT WHEN I SIGNED IT. I SOLD THE RIGHTS TO THE NAME WITHOUT REALIZING IT."

"I'm so sorry," Larthia said. "What can we call you?"

"IN THE SECOND MOVIE THEY CALLED ME DANIEL."

"What are you doing in LA?" Éduard asked. "Aren't you from Chicago?"

"WE SHOT THE THIRD MOVIE HERE. I WAS TECH-NICAL CONSULTANT ON ALL THREE. I STAYED ON HOPING TO MAKE A DEAL FOR MORE SEQUELS. I'VE HAD SOME INTEREST IN A REBOOT."

"Good luck with that, I mean that. Your first movie was quite good, taking on social issues and all. The other two –"

"I KNOW. THE THIRD ONE WAS DIRECT TO DVD."

"I no like third one at all," Lazarko said. "No offense."

"NONE TAKEN. IT ONLY HAS THIRTEEN PERCENT ON ROTTEN TOMATOES."

"What have been doing all these years?"

"I DO STAND-IN FOR TONY TODD, WHO PLAYED ME IN THE MOVIES. I'VE DONE SOME ONSCREEN WORK. ODD JOBS, DRIVING, LIKE NOW."

"Eviscerated anyone with your hook recently?"

"I GAVE THAT UP. IT GOT OLD. HERE WE ARE."

The escalade stopped. "Nice meeting you," Larthia said as they all got out. The car drove away. The building they stood in front of was two stories tall, with no windows. It was built of pinkish-colored brick, and a parking lot next to it had a handful of cars. It cast a shadow that protected the vampires from the setting sun.

"Are we supposed to go in?" Éduard asked.

"Somebody sent the car for us," Larthia said. "We should accept their invitation."

"Don't worry," Lazarko said. "I can kill them if we don't like."

"Good idea, Laz," Gary said. "Kill everyone, why don't you."

In a row of glass doors, one was open. Éduard led the way through it. "Hello?" he called out in the large area inside. Inside, all the doors except the one that was open were barred with steel beams. Zombie-proofing, Éduard assumed.

"It's a movie theater."

Larthia was right. There was a counter where candy was once displayed. Behind it a large popcorn machine sat, devoid of popcorn. Two sets of swinging doors led to the theater. The room was empty, but clean. Someone took care of it.

The door closed behind them. A heavy lock clunked into place. Éduard was startled, and turned to look. The door was mechanical.

"Helooooo," Éduard called again.

"Over here!" The voice sounded amplified.

The werewolf and vampires followed the sound toward the concessions counter. They still didn't see anyone. "Is anyone here?" Larthia shouted.

"I said over here!"

Something moved on top of the counter. When he got close enough, Éduard realized that a group of small figures stood on the glass where Milk Duds, Junior Mints, and Sno-Caps were once sold. The top of the counter was a little higher than waist high for the vampire.

"Who are you?"

The seeming leader of the group, a fellow who stood about six inches tall, held a microphone made to fit his hand, with a wire attached to it that led behind the counter, probably to an amplifier. He was dressed in a collared shirt but no tie, and tiny blue jeans. The outfit would have fit right in on the West Side of LA. He had pointed ears. The group around him all wore clothing that would look normal on any human with the money for popular fashion.

The figure with the microphone was black. Some of the other pixies were too, but some were white or Asian.

"You're pixies? Forgive my ignorance, but I thought pixies were European."

"You think we're all white, huh? Are all vampires white?"

"Of course not, we exist in every part of the world."

"Same with us. Got any other racist comments to make?"

Éduard felt flustered. "No, no. Sorry."

"So what did you want to talk to us about?"

"May I ask something?" Larthia said. "How did you know we were coming?"

"The fairies put you on Faebook." The pixie gestured and a female of his species brought him a pixie-sized laptop. "There's quite a discussion of whether this zombie apocalypse you talk about is real or a hoax."

"We're on Facebook?" Éduard asked.

"Faebook. It's like Facebook, but for fairies and pixies and elves and so forth."

"I can kill these little peoples easy," Lazarko said. "If you want."

"No, Lazarko, and I mean it." Éduard turned back to the pixie. "I got the idea from the fairies that you are their enemies."

The pixie shrugged his tiny shoulders. "Well, they control the fairy dust market on the north side, and we control the pixie dust market on the south side."

Éduard decided not to ask what the difference was between fairy dust and pixie dust. They both sounded dangerous. "So basically, you're rival gangs?"

"You mean like the Bloods and the Crips?"

Éduard felt a surge of hunger. "Did you say blood? Do you have any?"

"Bloods, the gang. Get a grip, vampire."

"Sorry." Éduard tamped down the lust for both blood and flesh. "Can you help us?"

"What's in it for us?"

"Well, things going back to normal. Humans not eating each other. You know."

"We been around before humans came. We can survive without them."

"I see you're wearing human-style clothing, you have a laptop. How about a cell phone?"

The little man pulled out a teeny tiny device. "Apple Seed ɪɪ. Besides the pixie dust, we make a lot of human stuff in pixie sizes."

"So you like the way things were. We're hoping to end the zombie apocalypse."

"Not all of us believe this zombie apocalypse stuff. A lot of fairies on Faebook think you made it up."

"Speaking of fairies, what do you know about this?" Éduard took the fairy jar out of his pocket and set it on the counter.

"Is that who I think it is?"

"The queen of the fairies, in a jar that no one can open. The fairies say you put her in there and sold her to a necromancer."

"I know the queen is missing, the fairies talk about it on Faebook. But we didn't have anything to do with it."

"Who did?"

The male pixie shrugged. "Can't help you."

"Who's in charge here? Could they help?"

"We have a king. Normally I'd say ask him. But..."

"I'm sure I can make him see reason."

"Don't be too sure. The king is, well, it's hard to explain."

"Can I talk to him?"

"Sure, but...you know pixies are named after wood or pieces of wood? I'm Anthony Oak, that's Susan Branch."

The female pixie waved.

"Hello," Éduard said.

Anthony Oak said, "We call our leader King Chestnut."

"Why do you call him that?"

"Because he's a nut."

CHAPTER TWELVE

S USAN BRANCH SHOWED EDUARD, LARTHIA, LAZARKO and
  Gary to their quarters for the night. Susan asked to sit
on Éduard's shoulder, so she could talk to him while
directing him. The room she took the vampires to was probably the manager's office from the building's movie theater
days, but instead of a desk and office chairs, there were two
bunkbeds, a small table with a clock radio on it, and two
folding chairs.

"A little Spartan, but it will do," Éduard said.

"We let our human helpers stay here sometimes."

"You don't have a human here that we could, uh, talk
to?" Larthia asked.

"We like our human helpers," Susan said. "No feeding
on them."

"Just a little," Éduard said. "We don't have to kill them."

"Can I have separate room?" Lazarko asked. "They are
my friends but I don't want any sleep feeding."

"We wouldn't do that!" Larthia said. She looked pretty
hungry, but Éduard knew she would keep her fangs to

herself. He wasn't so sure about his own behavior. He craved both blood and flesh.

"I don't sleep," Gary said. "I'll wake you up if anyone gets bitey."

This arrangement seemed agreeable to all. Susan asked to be placed on the floor outside the door. A pixie-sized car, in fact an exact replica of a Mercedes convertible, down to the logo on the grill, waited for her.

Éduard put Susan down. She waved and started to get in the car.

"One more thing. Did we really walk through fairyland for a week? It seemed like a couple of hours." He bent way down to hear her reply.

"That's fairyland for you. We pixies like the real world. Bye!" She sat in the car and it drove away.

There wasn't much to do but rest. "Top or bottom?" he asked Larthia.

"Here? With Lazarko and Gary watching?"

"Bunkbed, darling. Which do you want?"

"Oh. Can we both fit in one? We haven't snuggled since this all started."

"I can always use a good snuggle, my dear." Éduard lay in a bottom bunk and Larthia draped herself over him.

"Awesome!" Gary said. "Vampire love!"

"Just sleeping," Éduard said. He closed his eyes. It did feel good to have her pressed against him. He still had trouble getting to sleep. Hunger filled him, visions of spurting veins and strips of tender human flesh occupied his thoughts.

"Turning out the lights," Lazarko said. "Gary, watch them."

The last thing Éduard heard before blacking out was "Will do, no doggie snacks tonight."

"Wake up!" An amplified voice shouted.

Éduard opened his eyes and saw Larthia looking at him. She seemed as startled as he was. They both sat up and saw Anthony Oak standing on the platform of a miniature vehicle like the ones that workers use to hang signs or change light bulbs in large public spaces. At its furthest extension, Oak was almost at the chest height of an adult human. Once again he had a microphone and amplifier. "Breakfast!" he shouted. "Not the helper!"

A human woman came into the room with a tray. She was an older black woman in a nice dress. The tray had two glasses of red liquid and a raw steak on a plate. "Cattle blood for our vampire guests and meat for the werewolf."

"What, no spiritual fulfillment for the spirit?" Gary asked from near the ceiling.

"Feel free to browse our library," Oak said.

The woman put the plate on the table and left, looking back a little fearfully. Oak used some controls on the vehicle to back it out of the room. The door closed.

Larthia quickly drained one of the glasses, then made a face. "Not as good as human, but it will keep me going."

Éduard hesitated. The glass of blood looked good, but the meat...he salivated at the thought of ripping into it and consuming it.

"I'm not a wolf all the time," Lazarko said. "In human form I prefer cooked meat."

"I'll take it!" Éduard snatched up the steak and sank his teeth into it. He chewed off a big hunk and felt the juices flow down his throat. He was almost done with the meat before he noticed Larthia, Gary and Lazarko staring at him in shock.

"I saw you eat all that raw chicken, but I didn't want to say anything," Gary said.

"Dear," Larthia said, "you did tell me...but this doesn't seem right. You're a vampire."

"I know." Éduard looked down, unable to meet his lover's eyes. "Ever since I was bitten, I have these cravings."

"You are zombie?" Lazarko said, then burst into laughter. "You are vampire zombie!"

"Vampzom," Gary said. "That was your preferred term, wasn't it?"

"You two talked about this?" Larthia asked.

"Just after I was bitten." Eduard still couldn't look up. "I thought it was a joke at the time."

The door opened again. The helper lady said, "It's time."

The meeting of the pixies assembled in the former movie theater. The screen was gone, a mighty throne taking its place on the stage. Pixie-sized theater seats filled the large room, and thousands of pixies filled the seats. A small section of seats for humans sat on a wooden platform near the back. Pixie-sized cameras focused on the throne, and images of it were shown on both pixie-sized and human-sized monitors throughout the auditorium.

Éduard sat next to Larthia in the human section. The helper lady and some other helpers sat in other seats. Lazarko sat behind the vampires. Gary floated up toward the high ceiling and came back with observations.

"They have a TV control room up in the old projection booth. They must be broadcasting this."

After a few minutes the house lights went down. A spotlight from the back shone on the throne. A loud voice announced, "Pixies, people, vampires, werewolf and ghost, we are proud to present the royalist of royalty, King Chestnut!"

The crowd applauded wildly. A pixie strode out from

behind the throne and climbed the stairs to get to the seat at the top. He waved. The cameras showed him in closeup.

"Thank you, thank you everyone." The king sat on the throne. "Do I look good on all these TVs or what?"

The crowd applauded again.

"I know, I know I look good." The little man waved his hands every time he talked. "Okay," he said, his voice amplified loudly throughout the room. "Enough about me. I am the best king, though, right? I have royal genes, you know."

"Your majesty," another voice came over the speakers. Anthony Oak. "We have a very important matter to discuss." Oak walked out next to the king, microphone in hand.

"Yes, of course, really important king stuff. Stuff that only I can solve."

"Yes, your majesty. I outlined everything in the briefing book I sent you."

There was a pause. On the screens the king could be seen to look around, darting his eyes back and forth. "Why don't you tell the folks about the stuff? I have a dry throat. Get me some water."

A young male pixie rushed to the throne with a glass of water. Anthony Oak turned to the assembled crowd. "Yes, sir. The most important item on our agenda today is whether to help the vampires Éduard and Larthia, the werewolf Lazarko, and Gary the Ghost to find the cause of the zombie apocalypse and perhaps a way to end it."

King Stump drank some water. "The what now?"

"Zombie apocalypse? Humans coming back from the dead, eating each other?"

"I don't like shows like that. I like reality shows, with real reality, like *Thomas the Tank Engine.* Whoo whoo!"

"Of course, your majesty. Right now, I'm afraid, the

undead humans eating each other thing is reality. All over the world."

"Remember the one where Sir Topham Hatt was mad at Thomas?"

"A favorite, sir. But you can help guide Thomas safely into the station."

"I like the sound of that."

"Just let us help our new friends, and take all the credit for yourself, and you will be the best king of the pixies we ever had."

"I'm already the best king of the pixies ever. They know that." Chestnut held his hands out to the crowd, which roared in approval.

When there was quiet again, Oak said, "Then you would be the bestest best king ever."

"Yes! I am the bestest better best king! I will put out a royal decree today!"

"To help end the zombie apocalypse," Oak said.

"Whatever! As long as I'm the best!"

"Yes, your majesty."

King Chestnut stood up and held his arms high in triumph. Then he descended the stairs and disappeared behind the structure. The lights went up. Pixies started to leave the theater in neat lines.

"Stay in your seats," the black helper lady said to the vampires and werewolf, "so you won't step on anybody."

Gary drifted close. "That was...quite a show. I'm glad humans don't have any leaders like that."

When the crowd was gone, Anthony Oak came down one aisle in his lift truck. "There's an art to dealing with him," he said when he got close.

"Your populace seems to love him," Gary said.

"In the dark you can't see who's clapping. We play recorded applause. He doesn't know the difference."

"Did you tell him about the fairy queen in the jar?"

"You've seen him, do you really think he knows anything? Anything at all?"

Éduard shook his head. "No. So the pixies are going to help?"

"We'll do what we can. I've already posted on Faebook that every supernatural creature should try to come up with some magic, or technique or something to get rid of the zombies."

"I appreciate it, Mr. Oak. I wish I knew what to do next."

"Keep talking to everyone. Have you tried the elves? The dwarves? The gods? The Writers Guild of America West?"

"No, I guess we have some more recruiting to do."

"I suppose I could try all the ghosts I know," Gary said.

"I should maybe go to Werewolves Association meeting, LA Chapter."

"Can you think of anyone else, dear?" Éduard asked Larthia.

"I did talk to a nice gentleman one day at Starbucks. He said he was an important film director."

"You were talking to a man? Should I be jealous?" Éduard asked.

"No, no, I was seducing him into meeting me someplace more private so I could suck his blood, but he said he had to get back to directing a movie."

"Everybody in LA is directing a movie."

"Yes, I'm sure. His was called something like Ex-ampular."

"*Exemplar?*" Éduard laughed. "Did he also direct *Lusitania? The Dominator?*"

"Why yes. John Carnahan, that was his name."

CHAPTER THIRTEEN

"H E'S ONE OF THE MOST FAMOUS MOVIE DIRECTORS IN the world, dear," Éduard said.

"Really?"

"I asked you to go see *Examplar* with me but you said you had some laundry to do."

"Blood stains have to be washed quickly or you'll never get them out."

"Everyone was talking about it. Green aliens, floating mountains, a trite plot about colonialism stolen from better movies?"

"You know I'm not much for fantasy movies."

"You watch all those vampire and zombie movies with me."

"Well vampires are real, and now we know zombies are too."

Éduard had to admit that she had a point. "How about *The Dominator,* starring Arnim Blackenovum? Or *Dominator Two, Day of Judging*? Not to mention a string of studio product that Carnahan didn't direct."

"I've heard of that. Didn't someone in that say 'I will return?'"

"Yes, and he was Governor of California for eight years."

"Oh, him. Yes, of course."

"I liked *Lusitania*," Gary said. "The made-up story of two people swapping spit during the true story of a ship being torpedoed and sunk during World War One. I loved the romance, though I had to imagine they were both guys."

"Bah," Lazarko said. "Carnahan is hack. Give me Michael Bay any day. Everything goes boom."

"Well," Anthony Oak interjected, "you guys think about any contacts who might help. I have to go tell the king that he just made the best speech ever in the history of the world."

"You liked the speech that much?" Éduard asked.

"I tell him that after every speech."

"Can I get on this Faebook?" Éduard asked.

"Sure. I'll send a human-sized laptop to your room. Susan will help you." Oak drove his platform vehicle away.

Éduard, Larthia, Lazarko and Gary left the auditorium and returned to the room with the bunk beds. In a few minutes a human helper came in, this time a teenager with light brown skin. He carried a laptop and Susan Branch rode on his shoulder. The young man put them both down on the table.

"Thanks, Julio," Susan said.

"You are going to play on computer?" Lazarko asked. "Is boring. Hey kid, where can I get some food?"

"I'll show you," Julio said. He and the werewolf left the room.

"So," Éduard said. He sat in a chair and looked at the closed laptop. "How do you turn this thing on?"

Susan stood next to the little computer and looked puzzled. "First you open it up."

"Good," Éduard said. "Good to know." He picked the laptop up and examined it on all sides. "How do you do that?"

"You've never used a computer before, have you?"

"When I was born, a quill pen was the height of information technology."

"You use video equipment all the time, dear," Larthia said. "I'm sure you can do this."

"Put it down," Susan said. When the laptop sat on the table again, she pointed to the front edge of it. "Just lift the screen off the keyboard."

"I don't see a screen."

"The top part."

Éduard pulled up on the top and the machine separated into a screen and a keyboard, hinged in the middle. "Oh, I see."

"Push that button." Susan stood on the lower part of the computer so she could point at the keyboard. When Éduard pushed the button, the screen lit up. "That wasn't so hard, was it?" the pixie woman asked.

"Physically no, but your sarcasm cuts me to the quick."

"Sorry." She didn't sound sorry.

"So now I can get on Faebook?"

"Just type 'Faebook dot biz' into Giggle."

"You want me to giggle?"

"Giggle is a search engine, made by a pixie tech company."

"I'm not searching for engines."

Susan sighed. "It's a thing that helps you search. There are millions of sites on the Magicnet."

Larthia asked, "Magicnet?"

"Sure. You think humans are the only ones with high tech? The supernatural world has its own internet, cell phone service, even satellites. They all run on magic."

"Pixies are part of this?"

"Part of it? We run most of it. Spellicon Valley is full of pixie-run companies."

Éduard thought of asking more about Spellicon Valley but decided against it. He used both index fingers to carefully type "Faebook dot biz" into the box that Susan pointed at.

"You don't type 'dot.'"

"You said Faebook dot biz."

"Dot isn't the word dot, it's a period."

"Well tell me what you mean." Éduard typed "Faebook . biz."

"It's all one word. No spaces."

"Why didn't you say that?"

Susan shook her head. "I thought young people were good at technology."

"Young? I was born before the United States of America was a gleam in George Washington's eye."

"I have been around since the first humans walked the earth."

"You don't look a day over a million." Éduard typed the correct address.

Susan smiled. "Now press enter."

"I enter the computer? More magic?"

"No, you press the key that says 'Enter' on it."

The vampire read all the keys and found the right one. He carefully pushed it. The screen flashed and a new page came up. It showed a number of boxes with writing in them.

"This is my page," Susan said. "If I write something, all my friends will spread the message."

"What should we say?" Larthia asked.

"You two decide. Personally I think you should let the zombie thing run its course."

"And let all the humans die?" Éduard asked. "You don't need human blood to survive."

"There would still be cattle, horses, dogs."

"Eeew," Larthia made a face. "It's not the same. Anything but human blood tastes bad, and it doesn't sustain us for long."

"Interesting," Susan said. "Zombies only eat humans. They must think other creatures taste bad too."

"In *The Walking Dead* they seem to like horses." Éduard played around with pressing the letters on the keyboard.

"In *Survival of the Dead,*" Susan said, "some humans try to teach zombies to eat horses."

"I don't know that movie."

"Romero movie, just a few years before he died. May he rest in undeath. Two families on a small island fight zombies and each other."

"Oh. George was the Godfather of zombies," Éduard said. "But I gave up on him after *Diary of the Dead.* He tried to do the lost footage thing. It didn't work."

"I saw that with Éduard," Larthia said. "Definitely not Mr. Romero's best."

"*Survival* had some funny moments."

Gary drifted into the conversation from wherever he had been floating. "You're missing the best zombie movies. There's *Dead Dykes of Death Row, Blowjobs of the Dead,* and *Donny Does the Dead.*"

"Are those real?" Susan asked.

"Sure. Eating people can have a whole different meaning on gay porn websites."

"Er, thanks," the pixie said.

"You're welcome. Then there are gay ghost porn websites, and gay goblin porn websites, and gay gargoyle porn websites..."

"Is he kidding?" Susan asked Éduard.

"You never know with him," Éduard said. "Can we get back to writing something on Faebook?"

"What do you want to say?"

"I think we should ask all the supernatural creatures of LA to meet," Larthia said. "One of them must have an idea what to do about the zombies."

"A real life meeting? Why not just discuss it on Faebook?"

"Something about being together physically brings out ideas, I think. The Vampire Council has regular meetings."

"That last one was really productive," Gary said with a roll of his ghostly eyes.

"Merde," Éduard said. "We missed the meeting on Friday. We were supposed to report back."

"Oh yes, we were somewhere in fairyland on Friday."

"Dracula won't be happy with us," Éduard said. "Oh well, there's nothing we could have told them."

"Where in LA would be a good place to meet?" Larthia asked.

"The heart of supernatural Los Angeles is where the ancients dwell."

The two vampires waited for Susan to elaborate.

"You know, where the spirits of creatures have gathered

for thousands of years. Mammoths, saber tooth cats, megafauna of all kinds."

"Oh," Éduard said. "You mean the La Brea Tar..."

"That place is the pits," Gary said. "Literally."

"That's the supernatural heart of LA?"

"Of course." Susan looked surprised. "You must have felt the ancient power there."

Éduard looked embarrassed. "I've been meaning to go, but you know. Angelenos don't go to the tourist traps."

"We did plan to go once," Larthia said, "shortly after all those fossils were discovered. But then something happened and we decided to stay home for a while."

"What happened?"

"World War I."

"I see. So what do you want to put in the notice?" Susan asked.

"What do you think of this?" Eduard read what he had typed. "Vampires! Fairies! Ghosts! Werewolves! All the supernatural creatures of LA! Come help us plan how to end the zombie apocalypse! La Brea Tar Pits this Friday night just after sunset. Bring your own refreshments!" He looked up to see how his friends would react.

"That's terrible, dear," Larthia said.

"What? It's snappy and gets right to the point."

"She's right," Gary said. "Sounds like a grade school birthday party invitation."

"Let me." Larthia leaned over the keyboard, her hair brushing Éduard and her smell enveloping him, a combination of lilacs and fresh blood. She typed on the keyboard.

"Attention supernatural residents of Los Angeles: In response to the recent crisis involving zombies destroying the world, we feel that we, the undead and otherwise magical creatures of this city are uniquely qualified to devise a plan to reduce and/or mitigate the damage and perhaps return things to normal. Meeting at the La Brea Tar Pits just after dark two days from now."

"That's worse," Gary said. "It's like a meeting announcement in an accounting firm."

Larthia looked at Éduard. "It isn't that bad, is it?"

"Wha–? Sorry, I fell asleep."

Larthia scowled at him.

"It needs to be snappy and informative at the same time," Susan said.

A crashing sound of breaking glass came from the lobby. Éduard looked up. "What's that?

"We'd better see," Larthia said. "We'll finish this when we come back." The two vampires left the room.

"Type for me," Gary said.

"What?" Susan asked. "I should go see what that noise is too."

"C'mon, while they're gone I'll write the perfect message."

"I'm six inches tall. Do you want me to dance on the keys like Tom Hanks in *Big*?"

"Do it on your pixie phone."

Susan grumbled but brought out her phone and opened Faebook. "Okay."

"Party party party! Sunset to who knows when, La Brea Tar Pits, in two days! Everyone magical, undead, gods, demigods, trolls, gnomes, fairies, pixies, and whatever you are! Food and booze free!"

"How are you going to pay for the food and booze?"

"I'm not, once they see it's a serious meeting, they won't want it."

"Or they'll riot."

"Just send it."

"We'd better wait for Éduard and –"

Screaming erupted from the lobby. More things crashed. The door of the bedroom slammed open and Lazarko in werewolf form burst into the room. "Zombies break in! We must go!"

"Looks like it's my message or none," Gary said.

Susan nodded and pressed "Post."

CHAPTER FOURTEEN

THE LOBBY WAS A MADHOUSE. THE PROTECTIVE STEEL beams on some of the doors had been taken down. Zombies crashed through the glass. One of the human helpers lay on the ground with a zombie slurping her intestines like spaghetti. Another one held off a zombie with a stool from behind the concession stand, but he had a large bite on his cheek so he would join the hordes of the undead soon.

Pixies ran all over the place, and Éduard was surprised to see that the zombies were picking them up by the handful and gulping them down like snack chips. Most were gone in two bites.

A surge of hunger filled the vampire. Hunger for flesh. Could pixies sate this new appetite? He tried to fight the urge.

Lazarko deposited Susan on Larthia's shoulder, then waded into the zombies with glee, ripping them apart with teeth and claws. A large woman in a mail carrier uniform tried to bite him, but he put his fist through her face before she could.

"Darling, what should we do?" Larthia asked, coming up to Éduard and touching him on the arm. Susan held onto the vampire's hair with one hand and her phone with the other.

"You won't believe this," Susan said. "King Chestnut had his personal helpers open the doors."

"What?" Éduard yelped. "Why would he do that?"

"He thinks we should be friends with the zombies. Some of us have wondered if he likes them too much."

Éduard gulped and looked away. He suddenly realized that Susan looked delicious. "What can we do?"

"Get to the meeting," Gary said, floating close. "If all the supernatural creatures of LA can't come up with a plan, no one can."

"We didn't send the message."

"I did, with Susan's help."

Éduard glanced at Susan. His stomach rumbled. He resisted, because Larthia wouldn't approve and because he was afraid that, like Lay's potato chips, he couldn't eat just one. "Look!" Éduard said. "It's daylight out. How can we go anywhere?"

The shattered doors let in the midday sun. Even the light that reflected off the floor and walls made Éduard uncomfortable.

"Go through the theater!" Susan shouted.

"Lazarko! This way!" The vampires, one pixie, one werewolf, and one ghost, made their way toward the theater doors. They pushed a door open and entered. The large room was designed to be dark, but it did not keep out zombies. A tall black man in a nice suit chased a human helper down one aisle, while in the other aisle a neighborhood kid in basketball shorts and one expensive athletic shoe looked for pixies under the seats. He only had one shoe because the other foot was missing. He dragged his leg and supported himself on protruding bones to take a step.

"Behind the throne," Susan said. Everyone made their way to the front of the room and climbed a short set of stairs on one side of the stage. They passed the regal seat of power were King Chestnut had spoken.

Susan pointed, so Larthia followed her finger. On stage right, the top of a spiral staircase rose from the floor. Éduard looked around and didn't see any zombies.

Then a body fell with a splat from high above. "They're on the catwalk!" Susan said. The body, a fat man in pajamas, pushed himself off the floor and looked up. His face was as flat as a pancake, nose completely pushed in from the fall and mouth a line that leaked blood. He was closest to Éduard, who had no idea what to do. The zombie opened its mouth and several loose teeth flowed down his chin in a river of blood.

Ordinarily so much blood would smell to Éduard like a gourmet meal, but what came out of the zombie smelled foul, as if it came from hell itself. Nor did his desire for flesh react well to the dead man, though the zombie had plenty of flesh that would normally smell like Thanksgiving dinner. Éduard felt a little sick at the thought of drinking and/or eating any part of this man.

"Are you going to kill it?" Gary asked.

"Me?"

"You're the closest."

"How?"

"The teeth are all busted out," Gary said. "He can't bite. Just reach in and rearrange his brain."

The zombie took a halting step toward Éduard, who grimaced and did what Gary suggested. Putting his hand in the wet orifice was unpleasant and cold. He used his vampire claws to dig deep until the eyes of the thing went blank. Éduard pulled his hand back and the zombie fell to the ground.

Éduard's hand had pieces of brain on it. He frowned with disgust. "Lazarko could have done that."

"It was fun watching you," the werewolf said, grinning.

"Down the stairs," Susan said from her perch on Larthia's shoulder. Éduard followed the others down the spiral staircase and went around and around several times, finding himself in a large room with cement walls and fluorescent lighting.

It was some kind of workshop, with tables along the walls, power tools here and there, and a group of humans working on something in the center.

"There you are!" an amplified voice boomed. Anthony Oak, on his pixie-sized lift vehicle, rolled toward the vampires. "We aren't quite ready, but with the current situation it will have to do."

"What will have to do?" Éduard asked.

Anthony turned his vehicle around and rolled toward the people working in the center of the room. Éduard followed him and saw that they were working on a car.

"Is that a car or a Hot Wheels toy?" Gary asked.

"It's all we had on short notice," Anthony Oak said.

It was one of those tiny urban cars with only two seats, mounted on huge truck tires. "It's called a SmartForTwo." Anthony waved his pixie hand toward the vehicle. "We have modified it so it will roll over zombies, or even piles of zombies. You should be able to go over fallen trees or rubble also."

"A monster Smart Car," Gary said. "Never thought I would see that."

A female zombie tumbled down the spiral staircase, lay

quiet for a moment, then tried to stand. "There will be more of them," Anthony said. "You have to leave right now."

"It's daytime," Éduard said. "We can't go outside until night."

"We took a cue from a movie. Have you seen *Daybreakers*?"

It took Éduard a moment to remember the film. "Oh, vampires rule the world, and they drive around in cars that block UV light!"

"Right. It's also reinforced so zombies can't break the glass. I need you guys to do one thing before the big meeting at the Tar Pits."

"What's that?"

"Go to East LA. We need the cooperation of th quetzy gang."

"The who?"

The Hispanic creatures of the city. The gang is run by Quetzalcoatl himself. If we don't get their help half the supernaturals will stay home."

"How do I convince a god to come to the meeting?"

"Contact the duendes first. They're cousins of ours, sort of. Just don't let them trim your toenails. Now get in the car."

"Éduard and I never learned to drive," Larthia said.

"I drive!" Lazarko was still a werewolf, but more of a wolfman kind of werewolf. He had hands and could sit upright.

"Has anyone noticed that there are two seats and three of us?"

"I'll sit on your lap, darling," Larthia said. "I'm sure you won't mind."

"I'll float along, as usual," Gary said.

"This is where I get off." Susan Branch stood up on Larthia's shoulder. "Put me down."

"You sure?" Larthia asked. "Will you be okay?"

"We have pixie-sized tunnels all over the place. Zombies can't get into them. I'll be fine."

Larthia put the pixie onto a worktable. "It was nice to meet you."

Éduard had to resist a strong urge to pick the pixie up and cram her into his mouth.

"OPEN THE DOOR!" Anthony Oak bellowed through his amplifier. Much to the vampires' surprise, one side of the room moved up like a garage door, revealing a ramp. Lazarko jumped onto one of the massive tires and opened the door of the tiny car.

Éduard used his vampire powers to do the same on the other side. He sat in the one seat that was left, and Larthia gracefully settled onto him and pulled her legs in. "I think you'll have to close the door, dear," Éduard said. She did.

"Is fun! Driving tiny car with big wheels!" Lazarko grinned, canines flashing, and put the car in drive. They zoomed up the ramp much faster than they should have and emerged into bright sunshine on the street. Éduard instinctively threw his arm over his eyes, but didn't feel the pain of burning sunlight.

"It really does block UV," Larthia said.

"I knew that." Éduard put his arm down.

The car bumped wildly as Lazarko gleefully plowed into a group of zombies, knocked them down, and drove over them.

"Is like bowling!" Lazarko shouted.

"WHERE DO WE GO?" LAZARKO ASKED.
"East LA." Éduard peered through the windshield, trying to figure out where they were.

"Mmmm, Mexicans." Lazarko grinned.

"You like Mexican food?"

"Is what I said."

Talk of eating triggered Éduard's two hungers. Even Lazarko was beginning to look good.

"Why East LA, dear?" Larthia asked.

"Anthony Oak said we need to talk to the quetzy gang there. And contact something or someone called duendes."

"Never hear of this duendes."

"Me neither," Éduard said. "He said they are sort of cousins to the pixies. And not to let them trim our toenails."

Gary stuck his head through the roof. "There's a major blockage up ahead. An overturned semi and lots of cars."

Lazarko swerved to the left, taking a small street. Gary was left behind, his head disappearing from the car. The werewolf went around the block and back to the major street. Éduard could see the underside of the truck, which blocked the entire street.

"Hey!" Gary said, appearing again. "Give me some warning next time."

"Of course," Lazarko said. "Will be very careful to not annoy Mr. Gary." He rolled his eyes.

"I saw you roll your eyes, Lazarko."

"Was not secret, Mr. gay ghost."

"So that's it. Like your friend Putin you hate gay people."

"Me?" Lazarko sound fake offended. "I love gay people."

"Then you hate gay ghosts."

"I am very fond of the gay ghosts. I just hate you."

"If I could I would smack you right now..."

"Gentlemen," Larthia said. "Cut it out."

"No worries," Lazarko said. "I am behind Gary all the way. Just like his lovers. Ha."

"Stop!" Éduard gestured with both hands, trying to show how serious he was. It was awkward with Larthia in his lap. "We need to figure out how to get to East LA."

"Normally I'd take the 10 east," Gary said.

"Is coming up." Lazarko pointed to a green sign as they passed it.

The 10 freeway was elevated, with on and off ramps that took cars above the streets. When they got to the nearest on ramp, it was filled with stalled cars all the way up.

"Can't go that way," Éduard said.

"You think so?" Lazarko smiled. "You never see monster trucks on TV?" He moved toward the last car in the line.

"What are you doing?"

"You will see." Carefully putting one large tire next to a Nissan Sentra, Lazarko gunned the engine and got the tire to claw its way up onto the sedan. The Smartcar tilted sideways, throwing Éduard into his seat belt and making him clutch Larthia so she wouldn't fall onto the werewolf.

"Lazarko!"

"Hold on," the werewolf said. He got the second front tire up onto the Nissan, which made the SmartCar tilt backwards. Éduard was smothered in his lover's back as she fell on him.

"Oh!" Larthia cried out. "I hope you know what you're doing!"

Lazarko didn't say anything more as he got the rear wheels to dig into the steel of the Sentra and pull the car level, on top of the other car. Once again the vampires and the werewolf were able to look forward through the windshield.

"What the hell was that?" Gary said, sticking his head through the roof.

"Try to keep up, Mr. Ghost." Lazarko accelerated and moved the tiny car with its enormous wheels onto the next vehicle in line, then the next. Gary pulled his head out and disappeared. The car lurched back and forth as it climbed the roofs of each car then drove down onto the hoods and trunks of the next cars. SUVs were somewhat of a problem, but Lazarko managed to work the Smartcar up the on ramp to the freeway, which was four lanes of dead cars, as far as the eye could see, on both sides, east and west.

"Now we drive easy."

Easy wasn't really the word, but the little monster car was able to move slowly, on top of all the cars and SUVs that were stuck on the 10 freeway. Individual zombies walked between the cars, but the large wheels crushed any part of them that they encountered.

Gary entered again. "There are zombies in some of the cars. I wonder if any living people are still in some of them."

"Probably not," Éduard said. "They would have starved to death or died of thirst by now."

Gary shrugged his ectoplasmic shoulders and left the car.

"Darling," Larthia said. "Look."

"Hmm? Look at what?"

"The daylight world. So much light, we can see for miles. I haven't seen that since I was alive."

Once she had pointed it out, Éduard had to agree that it was amazing. He had forgotten how far one could see in daylight. A haze from fires hung over the city, but still he could see so much. "Clouds," he said, leaning forward and looking up through the protective glass. "I once took clouds for granted."

"You can see clouds at night," Lazarko said.

"It's not the same. They are so big and thick in daylight. Even when the moon is out at night, clouds don't look like this."

"I never thought of this before, dear," Larthia said. "Why can we go out in moonlight?"

"At night we can."

"Yes, but moonlight is reflected sunlight."

Éduard hadn't thought about that either. "I don't know," he had to admit.

"Vampires. Crazy," Lazarko said and laughed.

"That reminds me, Lazarko," Éduard said.

"What about?"

"You turn into a werewolf any time you want. And back to human. You don't worry about the full moon or wolfsbane blooming or anything."

"Family secret."

"We're all friends here. Come on, tell us."

"You tell anyone I rip you apart."

"Promise," Éduard said. Larthia agreed also.

The werewolf lifted a charm that hung from one of his gold chains. It had an unknowable mystic symbol on it. "Many times great grandmother make this. Has magic, I change any time I want."

Éduard was impressed. "I didn't know that was possible."

"Is many things vampires don't know."

Gary popped his head back in. "The way is clear up ahead, if you take it slow. Did I miss anything in here?" There was no response, so he left.

The monstrous SmartCar lurched and tilted its way toward East LA.

"How many scenes have you seen like this?" Larthia asked.

"Apocalypses?" Éduard said. "It is a popular theme. *Mad Max, Armageddon, Deep Impact, 2012* –"

"The theme of that one was boredom," Gary said. "Put me off John Cusack for good."

"You had a crush on John Cusack?"

"He had me at *Say Anything.* But by the time *2012* was over I wanted the world to end."

I think humans do want the world to end. They talk about it all the time. Remember the good old days of nuclear war movies? *On the Beach*? *Fail-Safe*? *Dr. Strangelove*?"

"We saw that together in New York," Larthia said. "We laughed so hard, but when we left the theater we almost expected the city to be a smoking ruin."

"There was the *Twilight Zone* episode. Burgess Meredith –"

"– and his glasses!" Larthia finished the sentence.

A group of zombies walked on top of the cars and turned

toward the car, as if it would stop for them. Lazarko gunned the engine and knocked them all down. One wheel lifted up as it drove over something, then went down suddenly. "Pop those heads like melons," Lazarko grinned.

"Hey," Éduard said, "*The Last Man on Earth*. Apocalypse AND vampires."

"I always liked Vincent Price. I had lunch with him once. He was doing vampire research for a guest appearance on *F Troop*."

"Vincent Price was on *F Troop*? As a vampire? Why didn't you tell me you met him?"

"It was just lunch. I don't tell you everything. There were two more versions of *The Last Man on Earth*, I think."

Still shocked, Éduard said, "Yeah, but in *Omega Man* the vampires were hippies, and in *I Am Legend*, which at least had the same title as the book, they were some kind of zombie things. Of course, *Last Man on Earth* was part of the inspiration for *Night of the Living Dead*."

"Really? I didn't know that. Uh oh."

"Uh oh what? You don't agree with me about George Romero's cinematic influences?"

"No, dear, about that." Larthia pointed ahead of them. Two semis had crashed into each other, and their bulk completely blocked the 10 freeway east.

Lazarko said something in Russian that was probably a curse word, but then everything in Russian sounded like cursing. He brought the SmartCar to a halt, each wheel resting on the roof of a different car.

Zombies noticed the car stopping, and drifted, moaning stereotypically, toward it.

Gary came through the roof and hovered in the little space behind the two seats. "What are we going to do now?"

"What do you mean we?" Lazarko growled. "You can float away any time your ghostly heart desires."

"I would never," Gary objected. "Well I suppose if you were dead and there was no reason to hang around. I would stay for a little while just to gloat over your corpse, Laz."

"We wouldn't be dead," Éduard said. "I mean, we are dead. You know what I mean."

"If enough zombies pounded on the car they could probably break the windows." Gary seemed to have thought about this. "If there's sunlight outside you would be really most sincerely dead. I'd hate to see my friends burst into flames."

"We'll just wait until nightfall and continue on foot," Larthia said.

"What about me?" Lazarko said. "We wait that long we will be covered in the zombies. I never make it."

The inside of the little car was silent for few moments. Then Gary looked up. "Something is coming." He floated through the roof.

"What?" Éduard asked. Larthia shrugged.

Gary came halfway in, smiling ear to ear. "You won't believe this."

The sound of flapping came from outside. Everyone looked and saw a house with peaked roofs covered in wooden tiles, and little narrow windows, lowering toward the congested freeway. The house had two chicken legs with taloned feet, that settled on the cars, which were crushed under the weight. The house also had chicken wings, which folded up on its sides.

Lazarko was the first to recognize who must have come to see them. His jaw fell open and he said, "Baba Yaga."

CHAPTER SIXTEEN

L ARTHIA TURNED HER HEAD IN AN AWKWARD SIDEWAYS angle and looked up through the windshield. "I know that house."

It was harder for Éduard to see, with his lover in his lap. He pushed his head forward and his eyes up. "Oh. The Spadena house."

"Where else you think Baba Yaga live?" Lazarko said. "She is legendary witch and show business executive."

"The house was designed by Hollywood art director Harry Oliver, a Hollywood art director," Éduard said. "It was originally built in 1921 to serve as the offices of a silent film studio, and was moved to its present location in Beverly Hills in 1934. The home was first owned by the Spadena family, who lent it their name."

"Thank you, Wikipedia." Gary rolled his eyes.

"I didn't know it could fly," Larthia said.

"Baba Yaga house always had chicken legs," Lazarko said. "But I never knew about wings."

Zombies started to cluster around the giant chicken feet of the house. One leg raised, then came down on a couple of them, crushing them into the car roofs and splattering blood on cars and other zombies. A couple more stomps cleared out the group of zombies closest to the legs.

Seemingly satisfied that zombies wouldn't bother it any more, the house settled down, legs crossing and then disappearing under it as it touched down. After a moment, the front door opened and a little old lady with stringy white hair under a headscarf peeked out.

"She looks just like my babushka." Lazarko smiled. "I mean, how babushkas are supposed to look. Mine was communist party apparatchik, wore dark suit always."

"Babushka?" Gary asked.

"Grandmother, old woman. The scarf is babushka, name attached to women who wear one."

The old woman waved and seemed to expect someone to get out of the car and go to her. "I talk to her," Lazarko said. He opened the door and jumped out. Éduard and Larthia pushed themselves against that other side of the car to avoid any sunlight that might come in. For a second the driver's seat was bathed in bright light and then the door slammed shut. The vampires relaxed.

Lazarko had reached the house by the time Éduard looked. The werewolf gestured toward the Smart Car and Baba Yaga, for that was who the woman had to be. They spoke in Russian, so what they said was unclear.

Gary, still squishing his ectoplasm into the seatless back of the car, said, "He's telling her you guys can't leave the car until nightfall. She is agreeing to help you."

"You speak Russian, Gary?" Larthia asked.

"And since she works for Disney, she can get me a date with Zac Efron."

"You're making it up," Éduard objected.

"Had you for a minute there."

Lazarko turned back toward the car, decapitating a female zombie in a McDonald's uniform along the way. He yanked the door open again and climbed in. Sunlight once again poured in. Larthia couldn't pull her left hand back fast enough and a puff of smoke came off of it.

"Sorry," Lazarko said, shutting the door.

"It'll heal." Larthia held her burnt hand with her other hand and winced.

"You didn't have to go," Gary said. "I could have gone without opening the door."

"You not Russian. We had a lot to talk about."

"Such as?" The gay ghost asked.

"She hate Putin too."

"Because he's an oligarch, a dictator in all but name, and a killer?" Larthia asked.

"He almost ban live action *Beauty and Beast* from his country. He put age sixteen and above rating on it."

"That doesn't sound like much..." Éduard inserted.

"Baba Yaga say kids are biggest market!"

"He did that," Gary said, "because there's a gay character in it. I for one applaud Disney for the courage to include him."

Éduard decided to cut to the chase. "Did you ask her about helping us?"

"Oh yeah," Lazarko said. "She's been keeping an eye on us since we used Wuber." He put on his seat belt. "Hold on tight."

Oh," Éduard said. "I forgot that the Wuber driver wanted me to ask Baba Yaga about a remake of her screenplay."

"Probably a question for a time when civilization has returned," Larthia said.

"I suppose," Éduard said. "How can she get us past these trucks?"

"I said hold on tight." Lazarko gripped the steering wheel as if he expected something to happen.

"The witch house is moving." Larthia pointed. Éduard looked and saw the famous house rise on its chicken feet. It made one hop toward the Smart Car and lifted one leg.

"What is it going to do?" The question was answered when the giant chicken foot clasped the car tightly.

"Whatever it is, I'm out of here." Gary slipped through the roof of the car.

A moment later the sound of giant chicken wings flapping was heard and the house, car and all, lurched into the air.

Éduard screamed. Larthia closed her eyes. Lazarko grinned. A sick feeling went through Éduard's gut as the car went up and down in the air. Then it felt like the car was falling.

The house put its feet down on the stalled cars on the freeway, past the blockage of the trucks. In just a second it picked up the car again and they sailed into the air again. "What is it doing?" Éduard moaned.

"Chickens only fly a little far, you know," Lazarko said. "It needs to go a little, stop, then go again."

"It's going to hop us from here to East LA?" Eduard's dual hungers surged to the fore, then the feeling that he needed to throw up both flesh and blood surged through him. He hadn't eaten either in quite a while, so his urge to vomit produced only a string of saliva that hung from his mouth.

The chicken house landed, flew, landed, flew, for longer than seemed possible. Larthia stroked Éduard's head and tried to soothe him. Lazarko seemed happy. "Is like Six Flags ride, but no lines! And free!"

"I can't imagine you at Six Flags," Larthia said.

"Oh yes, I take whole family. They love roller of the coasters!"

After what felt like an hour of short hops, the chicken house let go of the little car. It stood nearby for a minute, then jumped in the air and hopped away.

"Where are we?" Larthia asked.

Gary flew in through the roof. "You guys okay? That looked like a rough trip."

"Best roller coaster," Lazarko said.

Éduard just said, "Bleh."

The view out of the window was a large intersection. Cars were scattered around, some just burned-out hulks. Éduard saw something on a sign that he really didn't expect to see. "Dinosaur."

"Are you seeing things, darling?" Larthia asked. She was facing away from the sign and couldn't see it.

"Dinosaur," Éduard repeated. "It's a Sinclair station!"

Larthia twisted around. "You're right. I didn't know they still existed."

The gas station had several friendly green dinosaurs on different signs. Éduard remembered ads for Sinclair gas from decades ago, but was surprised to see one. It wasn't currently in service, because of the whole zombie apocalypse thing, and in fact a bread delivery truck had run into the store in the center of the station, breaking out several of the big windows, but it was still clearly a Sinclair gas station.

"Not the Mama! Not the Mama!" Éduard said.

"I don't think he's recovered from all the jumping," Gary remarked.

"You must remember," Éduard said. "*Dinosaurs*? Great show. Mr. Sinclair was the boss, he was named after this gas company. And the baby shouted 'Not the Mama!' and hit his dad with a frying pan."

. . .

"If you say so," Gary said. "So what are we going to do now?"

Lazarko started the engine. "Can drive."

"Yeah, but where?" Gary popped out of the car and was back in a flash. "We're on Soto Street. Must be Boyle Heights."

"I've never been in this part of LA before," Larthia said.

"It's actually an unincorporated area," Éduard explained.

"*Born in East LA*," Gary said. "Never saw that, but that's where we are."

"Cheech Marin was in *From Dusk Till Dawn*. Great vampire movie."

"If you like a gun in a guy's crotch, Éd," Gary said. "Which I do."

"Cut chatter. Where we go?" Lazarko asked.

It was late in the day. The sun was a large yellow ball over the more expensive side of town. Pretty soon the vampires would be able to get out of the UV-protected confines of the tiny car. There weren't any zombies on the street that Éduard could see.

"What's that smell?" Éduard's lust for flesh flared as he realized there was a delicious odor coming from nearby. The only possible source was a restaurant on the opposite corner. It was a small building with a few parking spaces around it. A sign on top said "¡Muy Bueno!" Blue awnings over an area with a few tables and chairs said "Preparamos Su Comida" and "Para Qualqier Evento."

"Smells like burning flesh," Larthia said. "Disgusting."

Éduard licked his lips. His stomach made a rumbling noise.

"Don't tell me you want that." Larthia made a face.

"I'm sorry, dear, I don't want to want it, but I do."

"Look." Lazarko pointed at the restaurant as lights came on inside. "Is someone there."

The sun sank behind a building to the west and shadow covered the street. "Let's check it out." Éduard opened the door of the SmartCar. He helped Larthia jump down. When he had his feet on the pavement he looked around. He still saw no zombies, and wondered why. The smell of cooking meat and activity in the restaurant should attract them like flies to shit.

Larthia got to the door of the Mexican restaurant first, and pushed where a sign said PUSH. The door didn't budge. The windows had curtains behind them, and the shadow form of a person could be seen moving about inside.

Larthia knocked on the door. The person inside paused.

"What do we do if they don't answer?" Éduard asked.

"Get in car and drive," Lazarko said.

"But where to?"

"Guys," Gary said from behind the vampires and the werewolf. "You might want to turn around."

Éduard glanced behind him. What he saw shocked him, and he gripped Larthia's shoulder to make her turn and look. Lazarko also followed the movement of the other two.

Surrounding the front of the restaurant, dozens of little men stared at the group. They were bigger than the pixies, maybe eighteen inches tall. They wore ragged pants but no shirts, and on each head there was a straw hat with a wide brim and a point at the top. They grinned widely, showing sharp teeth. They had a wild look in their eyes.

"We're in trouble," Éduard said.

CHAPTER SEVENTEEN

T HE DOOR OPENED AND A WOMAN'S VOICE SAID, "Adelante, niños. "

The large group of little men pushed forward. Éduard, Larthia, and Lazarko had to back up into the restaurant or be knocked over. Once inside, the little creatures ignored the vampires and the werewolf and walked toward the restaurant tables.

"Are those the duendes?" Larthia asked.

"They fit the description that Anthony Oak gave me."

"Do they taste good?" Lazarko said.

"I hope you're joking," Éduard said. "You eat one and the rest would tear us apart with those teeth."

"Joke a little. I am hungry enough to eat two horses."

Éduard had to agree, the smell of cooking meat made his stomach demand food. His vampire blood lust also flared.

"I am so glad I don't eat," Gary said after entering through the closed door. "At least, not food."

The restaurant was small, with ten tables. Some of the

duendes sat in chairs and some sat cross legged on the tables. They chattered in Spanish.

The woman who had opened the door came from the kitchen with a rolling cart, covered in bowls. She was about five feet five inches tall, with brown skin and dark hair. She put a bowl in front of each duende, and they ate whatever was in them by scooping the food with their hands and pushing it into their mouths.

The noise level in the small area was intense as the woman had to make several trips to the kitchen and back to supply each little man with food. Surprisingly, each one waited patiently. One reached to grab his neighbor's bowl, but the woman snapped, "¡Sé bueno!" and he pulled his arm back.

After distributing the last of the bowls, the woman noticed her uninvited guests. Her eyes widened and walked up to Éduard. "¿Quien eres usted?" Her question seemed clear, though the vampire spoke no Spanish.

"I'm Éduard, this is Larthia and Lazarko."

"Don't forget me, Éd." Gary smiled at the woman. "Muchos nachos, señorita."

The woman looked puzzled but stared hard at Gary. "Fantasma."

"Si," Gary agreed. "Estoy un ghost."

"You know Spanish, Gary? Or are you faking again?" Éduard asked.

"High school. "¿Donde esta la biblioteca?"

"¡No te quiero aqui!" She pointed emphatically at the door.

"I think she wants us to leave," Larthia said.

"That's pretty clear," Éduard said. The he spoke to the woman. "Can we get some food? He looked at Gary. "Do you know the word?"

"Comida," Gary said. "Tenemos mucho ambre." He mimed.

The woman shook her head. "I speak English, stupid people. I told you to go!"

One of the duendes hopped on top of her cart and bent his head toward the woman's. He spoke into her ear. All Éduard understood was the word "Faebook." When the little man finished she gave the vampires an appraising look. "You are them."

"Them?" Éduard asked.

"On Faebook, the vampires who want to end the plague of the dead."

"Why yes, we are."

"You are estupido."

"Excuse me?"

"There is no end. We live in el mundo de los muertes."

Larthia broke in. "We were sent to speak to Quetzalcoatl."

The woman stepped back when the name was spoken. A murmur went through the massed duendes.

"Do you want to tell a god that you sent us away?" Larthia asked.

"He will punish you for saying his name without reverence."

"Let's leave that to him, shall we? In the meantime, we need some food and rest."

The woman turned around and stalked off. She entered the kitchen, going right through the door without bothering to open it.

"I knew it!" Gary said.

"Knew what?" Lazarko asked.

"Did you get any smell off her?"

The vampires and the werewolf all shook their heads.

"She's a ghost! Or some kind of spirit."

"Gary," Éduard said, "she handled the cart and the bowls, all kinds of physical things. You go through everything."

"Ghosts that have been around a very long time can do that. She must be centuries old."

The woman appeared again, this time opening the door. She had a platter of food. "Sit," she said. She shooed duendes away from one of the tables.

"This smells delicious," Éduard said as he sat. There was a bowl of steaming meat and a pile of tortillas. Two open wine bottles were full of a dark red liquid and two wine glasses were next to them. The platter also held utensils and napkins.

"You are vampire, no? You do not eat."

"Oh, yes," Éduard said, looking embarrassed. "Of course. Is this blood?" He picked up one of the bottles.

"From beef. There are no living people here to suck on."

"That's fine, thank you," Larthia said. She poured herself a glass of blood. "Will you join us?"

"I do not eat either," the woman said, then went back to the kitchen.

"I do," Lazarko said, licking his lips. He spooned a large amount of the meat onto a tortilla, rolled it up and tore into it.

Éduard hesitated. He wanted that meat badly. He poured and gulped some blood, but watched the meat to make sure Lazarko didn't take it all.

"Go ahead, darling," Larthia said. "I know you want to."

"But what it if makes it worse? What if I become a zombie permanently?"

"It could help you hold off the craving to eat human flesh."

There was no way to know, but the meat smelled too good. Éduard followed Lazarko in making a large taco and biting into it. It was delicious.

A duende tugged at Larthia's dress. "Por favor," he said in a gravelly voice, "Please, may we clip your toenails?"

"You speak English?"

"Si, señorita. Yes, miss. We really enjoy clipping the toenails."

"Vampires nails don't grow. Perhaps Lazarko?"

"Keep little hands away from my toes, fingers or any part of me," the werewolf growled.

The entire group of duendes spoke at the same time. "We want to clip your toenails."

"Basta!" The woman came into the room. "No toenails! They are guests!" She came up to the group. "I am sorry, they always want to clip toenails. Do not let them, sometimes they take the whole toe."

"I'll remember that," Éduard said. "This food is delicious."

"I thought the vampires only drank blood."

"Oh, heh, yes, I'm a little different. This is very good beef."

"It is not beef, or at least not the meat of a cow."

"Really? Then what is it?"

"Sesos."

Gary burst out laughing.

"Gary?" Larthia said.

"I'm sorry," the ghost said between gasps of laughter. "This is hilarious."

"What?" Lazarko demanded. "What do I eat?"

"Sesos!" Gary laughed even louder.

"He's gone crazy."

"There must be some reason, dear," Larthia said. "Miss, what are sesos?"

"How you say in English?" the dark-haired woman said.

"BRAINS!" Gary shouted. "You're really a zombie, Ed! You're eating brrrrains!"

Lazarko shrugged and took another big bite. "Is good."

"Brrrrrains!" Gary said again, imitating *Return of the Living Dead* zombies.

If vampires could blush, Éduard would have been beet red. "It's not that funny, Gary."

"Brrrrains!"

Éduard put down his taco. He had lost his appetite. "Young lady, couldn't you have brought out beef? Or chicken? This is horrifying."

"You are picky when I give you food for nothing? I have no carne o pollo. There is the end of the world outside!"

"Well what do you feed your little friends then?" Éduard gestured to the duendes, who were raptly watching.

"My children bring me their food. I just cook it."

Gary stopped shouting "Brrrrains!" and said, "What food is out there that these little monsters would like?"

The woman smiled. "You did not see any of the zombies out there, did you? The whole neighborhood is wiped clean." She turned and entered the kitchen, once again forgetting to open the door first.

Éduard drank some of the cow blood straight out of a bottle, trying to reclaim his vampire nature. It was good, but the brain taco still called to him.

"Did she call these guys her children?" Gary asked.

"She did say that," Larthia said.

"Is she your mother? Tu madre?" Gary asked loudly.

The duendes all said, "No, no no no." Then one of them, probably the one who whispered in the woman's ear, but it was hard to tell them apart, came close and said, "She looked for her children for very long time."

"This sounds familiar," Gary said.

"Si, she lost two children very long ago. She has been looking ever since."

"I've heard a story like this." Gary looked interested. "Tell me more."

"When the muertos – zombies came, she found us on the street hunting them."

"And since you're small she thought you were children."

"Si, señor." The duende shrugged. "We did not mind, she cooked our food."

"What are you two talking about?" Éduard asked.

"There is an old story," Gary said. "A woman loses her children, or throws them in a river herself. She dies and haunts the river forever. Sometimes she steals living children and kills them."

"There was an episode of *Supernatural* that was a little like that."

"Not surprised, they have used every folktale ever told."

"She comes." The duende scrambled back to a table full of his friends.

The woman came in with a cart. "Time to clean up, children. Put your bowls on the cart."

"Miss," Éduard said. "You haven't told us your name."

The woman glanced at the vampire. "Maria."

"There's another name people call you," Gary said.

"I do not know what you talk about. Come on! Put your bowls here!"

"How about 'La Llorona?'"

Maria turned fast toward Gary and his friends, face melting into a skull, hands growing long, sharp claws. She hissed, a long tongue hanging out of her mouth. "Do not call me that," she said in a voice straight out of hell.

Then she shook her head and returned to her previous form. "Lo siento. I am sorry. I promised my therapist I would stop doing that."

CHAPTER EIGHTEEN

THERE WAS A SHORT SILENCE, THEN LARTHIA SAID, "Did you say therapist?"

"Yes, that's why I came to Los Angeles." Maria pronounced the city in the Spanish way, Los with a long o, then Anhaylays. "I decided to get grief counseling, along with anger management therapy."

"If your therapist was a human," Gary said, "he or she is probably a flesh-eating zombie now."

Maria nodded. "I know. But it doesn't matter. I don't need her anymore." A round of laughter went through the duendes. The woman spread her arms and broke into a huge smile. "I have found my children."

The straw-hatted, sharp toothed, toe-clipping horde of little monsters gathered around her. "Mama," they chanted in unison. "Mama, mama."

This spectacle made even a bloodthirsty and zombie-cursed vampire such as Éduard feel a touch of fear. He stood up and took a step back. Larthia did too. Lazarko stood, leaned toward him and whispered, "loco" in his ear.

When the chanting ended Éduard didn't know what to

say. He looked at his beloved. She raised an eyebrow, then turned to the crazy ghost. "So, ah, can you put us in touch with the quetzy gang? We need to talk to – you know who."

"This is not so easy," Maria said, looking a little more normal and a little less insane. "I can contact the gang, but you have to make them take you to Quetzalcoatl." She said the god's name with a great deal of reverence.

"That would be so nice of you, dear."

"You may not think so. The Qetzies are the worst gang in LA. They will not be kind to strangers."

"Let me worry about that," Lazarko said. "I can take a bunch of humans."

Maria smiled again. "It is not the humans I would worry about, Señor."

Before long, the duendes left the restaurant and the place became quiet. Lazarko said he needed sleep and curled up on the floor under a table. Night had arrived outside, the natural time for vampires to be awake. Éduard and Larthia didn't feel like sleeping even though they had not rested during the day.

Maria went to the kitchen and stayed there. Where an insane, killer mom-ghost spent her off hours was unknown and the vampires were happy to let it stay a mystery. Gary drifted here and there inside the restaurant, thinking gay ghostly thoughts.

"Did you ever think we would come so far?" Larthia asked. They sat at a table , with all the chairs except the two that they used upside down on the other tables. The duendes had cleared all the dishes and mopped the floor.

"What, to Boyle Heights?"

"No, silly," Larthia said. "In our search. We set out to find a way to end the zombie apocalypse. I thought we would just go to the vampire council meeting and go home. But we have met trolls, Chinese vampires, fairies, pixies, and now duendes and La Llorona."

"We aren't any closer to finding what we want to find."

Larthia put a hand on her lover's arm. "Do you really think we'll find it? I'm sorry, darling, I don't have much faith in this quest. I'm having a good time, though. It's a lot more interesting than sitting at home. It's like the old days, when we travelled and took blood whenever and from whomever we wanted."

"There won't be much blood to take if zombies eat all the humans."

"You can eat meat now, maybe that's a good thing. Maybe you can go on after –"

Éduard frowned when he realized why she didn't end that sentence. "After you're gone, you mean? After there is no food for you, and you dry up into a husk?"

Larthia looked down, not willing to meet his eyes.

"I don't want that," Éduard said. He tried to imagine wandering the Earth forever, fighting zombies for scraps of flesh. "No music, no parties, no sidewalk cafés, no..." He gripped the table hard when he realized the last thing.

"No movies?" Larthia asked.

"That's not what I was thinking."

"Yes it is, I know you."

"All right, but the thing I would miss most is you, dear."

"Awww." Gary appeared next to the vampires. "Romance. How boring."

"Can you drift off somewhere, Gary?" Éduard asked. "We need a moment."

"Even you can make it last longer than a moment, Ed. Try foreplay."

Larthia laughed.

"You thought that was funny?"

"Of course not, dear." Larthia smiled, despite her denial.

"Hmph." Éduard stood up. "I don't have to sit here and be insulted by a ghost."

Maria, La Llorona, swept into the room, her feet a couple feet off the floor. "It is time!" she declared in a spectral voice.

"Time for what?" Éduard asked.

"Time to shut up and listen to me, you stupid vampire."

"Now you get to be insulted by two ghosts," Gary said, grinning.

"He is here!" Maria said loudly. "Or, you will go there. Or maybe meet in the middle."

"What?"

La Llorona shifted to her skull face and shrieked at Éduard. The vampire sat. "Whatever you say, ma'am."

"Go now. Go and never return. Unless you do save the world. Then, we're open every day except Mondays. Sesos tacos are on special on Thursdays."

The door to the restaurant swung open by itself. Ghastly light came in from the street.

"After you, my dear." Éduard gestured to the door. Larthia proceeded him onto the street. Gary floated next to them. Outside, an army of duendes stood in a circle around the restaurant. Other, taller figures were among them.

The door opened again and Lazarko was pushed out. Maria's voice said, "Take your dog with you!"

"Hey!" the Russian said. "I am proud werewolf, of the Vetluga werewolves."

Maria followed Lazarko out and stood in the street. "Come," she said. "He will meet you."

Éduard walked forward into mist. He couldn't see the street or streetlights. Larthia came up behind him and took his arm. Gary hovered at his other side. "Very mysterious," the ghost said.

"The spirits brought here by the many people from Spanish-speaking lands everywhere will escort you." Maria waved toward the mist behind her.

"Who are they?" Éduard asked.

A duende stepped forward. "El cuco," he said, pointing to a shapeless form that emerged from the mist. The only thing distinct about him was a pumpkin head that had a hideous face carved upon it.

"We're supposed to be scared by jack-o-lantern?" Lazarko asked.

"El Silbon," the duende said.

A shirtless youth walked out of the mist and stood next to the pumpkin-headed man. He carried a sack over his shoulder that rattled as it moved. He put the sack down and Éduard could see fresh wounds on his back, as if he had been whipped.

Larthia tightened her grip on Éduard's arm. "The poor thing." The young man said nothing, but whistled several notes in a spectral pattern.

"La Ciguapa," Maria said. Another form came out of the mist.

"Kak krasivo!" Lazarko sounded like an online English to Russian translator. "This I like!"

The new form was a beautiful woman with long black hair that wrapped around her, acting as her only clothing. Éduard admired her beauty but noticed something odd. "Look at her feet," he said to Larthia.

"They point backward."

"Do not look her in the eyes," Maria warned. "She is known to lure men to her lair and kill them."

"That is not a problem." Lazarko gazed at a point about a foot lower than the spirit's face.

"La Cadejo," Maria said.

A pair of glowing red eyes appeared in the mist. A low growl filled the air. The eyes were those of a huge black dog.

"Nice puppy," Gary said.

Lazarko growled back at the dog, changing to his were-wolf form. He darted forward to meet the dog. The two supernatural canines circled each other, then smelled the other's rear.

"Last but not least in ferocious evilness," Maria said, "La Chupacabra."

The creature that came forward shifted in form, sometimes looking like a coyote with mange, sometimes like a disfigured wolf with long spines on its head and back, and sometimes reptilian.

Lazarko came back to stand next to the vampires. "That thing is too ugly for ass sniffing."

Gary floated toward the chupacabra, not afraid of being hurt by its claws or teeth. "I can buy the others, Maria," he said. "But the chupacabra has only been reported since nineteen ninety five. It's clearly a modern myth. This one can't even make up its mind what it looks like."

"You do not know, señor ghost." Maria crossed her arms, clearly irritated by the interruption. "Some witnesses say it looks one way, some say it looks like something else. It changes because it is described differently."

"And how does a story that owes more to the internet than reality become part of your big presentation here?"

"El chupacabra exists because people believe it exists."

Gary turned to Maria. "Huh. I have no counter argument

for that. Please continue." He floated back toward his friends.

Maria coughed, then threw her arms wide. "Now, come with me to see if the great Quetzalcoatl will bless you with an audience." She turned and walked, disappearing into the mist.

"I guess we're supposed to follow her," Éduard said.

"If you snooze you lose," Larthia said. She strode forward. The monsters formed a gauntlet and watched the vampires, werewolf and ghost pass them. Then they followed into the unknown.

The mist became so thick that Éduard couldn't see his friends around him. The sound of chanting started, soft at first, then louder and louder until he could hear nothing else. The mist began to clear, and Éduard found himself no longer on a street in Boyle Heights, but on a stone structure. The chanting came from thousands of people surrounding the structure.

It was a pyramid, with an elaborate temple on the flat surface on top. The people below wore simple clothing. The men had long capes and nothing else except loincloths. The women wore loose blouses and skirts. Next to the temple were several figures in much fancier costumes and head-dresses.

"They wear strange clothing," Lazarko said.

"I've seen stranger on an average Friday night in a West Hollywood gay bar," Gary said.

"Where are we?" Larthia asked.

"It looks like *Apocalypto*," Éduard said. "Mel Gibson directed it, it's about the Mayans."

The vampires stood on a platform lower down than the top of the pyramid. Steep stairs led far down to the ground and masses of people. One more flight of stairs led up to the top. One of the elaborately dressed figures near the temple saw them and pointed down. Several of them started down the stairs.

"Didn't they perform human sacrifice in that movie, darling?"

"Yes, but that might have been historically inaccurate," Éduard said. "It is thought the Mayans did a lot less of it than the Aztecs."

The priests – it was clear that's who they were as they got close – arrived at the lower platform and shouted in a language that Éduard did not understand. They tried to grab the arms of the group.

Lazarko switched to werewolf and snapped at them, making them back off. Éduard and Larthia merely used their vampire strength to pull away. The elaborately dressed men seemed afraid of Gary. He just laughed at them.

Éduard didn't get any human smell off these men, no rich blood or tasty flesh. As far as his vampire or zombie senses could tell, they weren't there.

A sound like many Hollywood movie explosions filled the air. Everyone looked up. There was a disturbance in the air, a ball of roiling gas. It expanded fast and something plummeted from the sky.

Just before hitting the top of the pyramid, the strange thing uncoiled into the form of a huge snake, covered in multi-colored feathers. It stopped in mid-air, striking a dramatic pose as unearthly music announced its arrival. The crowd roared. The priests raised their hands and shouted.

The music stopped, and the crowd noise subsided.

"Can I make an entrance or what?" Quetzalcoatl boomed in a godly voice.

CHAPTER NINETEEN

"WHERE ARE WE?" LARTHIA ASKED.

The splendid serpent looked down and became disappointed. "That's it? No applause? Not even a 'Yes you can make an entrance, your Godliness?'" He sank down to the stone surface and coiled there, his head raised and towering over the vampires and the werewolf.

"You're not the first god I've met," Larthia said. "I was born before Jupiter sat the throne of the gods. I tossed dice with Turms once, so that he would let me drink the blood of a small village."

"You never told me that," Éduard said.

Larthia shrugged. "It's not that great a story. The villagers tasted a little stale."

"I haven't heard of a god named Turms," the snake said.

"The Romans called him Mercury."

"Oh, that guy. Always running around. delivering messages. Not an easy god to talk to."

"So where did you say we are?" Larthia gestured at the pyramid, the temple, priests, and crowd of commoners.

"A little illusion I whipped up. I thought it would impress you."

Larthia crossed her arms, obviously not impressed.

"I think it's cool," Gary said. "It's like the Aztecs crossed with the Mayans crossed with an early episode of *Dr. Who.*"

"I didn't bother to make it specific. I am a deity of many Meso-American cultures. You can call me Kukulkan if you like."

"Kukulkan!" Lazarko laughed loudly. "Funny word. Kukulkan."

"It's the k sounds," Gary said. "Ask any standup comic."

"Anyway, Mr., uh, Quetzalcoatl, we came to see you because we are searching for a way to end the zombie apocalypse." Éduard tried to sound casual yet forceful. He didn't think he was doing it very well. "Anthony Oak of the pixies said we need your support to help bring all the supernatural creatures of LA to a meeting."

"I saw the Faebook post," the feathered serpent said. "Seems kind of stupid to me. How can anyone stop a zombie apocalypse? Why would they want to? I haven't seen so many mangled bodies since my heyday. In fact, it's put me off human sacrifice. There are so many bodies everywhere, it's a little much even for me."

"What happens when there are no living humans left?" Larthia asked. "No one to worship you? Or even remember you?"

The giant snake shrugged, which was quite a feat for a creature with no shoulders. "I don't know. I hadn't really thought about that."

"If we can get all the supernatural residents of LA to the meeting, maybe someone can come up with a plan," Éduard said. "Maybe there is a way to stop the zombie apocalypse. But we need everybody. The pixies said you control

East LA. We need you and everybody you can send to the meeting."

The feathered serpent seemed deep in thought. "I should just have my priests cut out all your hearts."

The priests perked up and moved toward the vampires.

"But no," the god said. The priests looked disappointed. "By the way, would that kill you vampires? Having your hearts cut out?"

"I haven't tried it, your godliness," Éduard said. "But I don't believe so."

Gary chimed in. "Unless you poke a pencil through the heart while it's outside the vampire. They do that in *From Dusk Till Dawn*."

"We don't need to give him any ideas, Gary," Éduard whispered to the ghost.

"Never mind," Quetzalcoatl said. "Just curious."

Éduard took the unbreakable jar out of his pocket. "Do you know anything about this?"

"I'm a snake. I don't eat pickles."

"It's the queen of the fairies, in a jar no one can open."

"You don't say." Quetzalcoatl lowered his serpentine head close to the jar. "How did she get in there?"

"We don't know."

The feathered serpent raised his head. "Nothing to do with me."

"Okay, thought I'd ask." Éduard tucked the jar back in his jacket.

"Tell you what."

"Yes?" Éduard asked.

"I'll come to the meeting, and bring all the creatures of the east side of L.A., if you guys pass a test."

"What test is that? Can you tell us about it?"

"Easier to show you," the feathered serpent said. He

leapt into the air and spread his multi-colored feathers. There was a snap sound and everything around Éduard, Larthia, Lazarko, and Gary changed. The Aztec/Mayan temple vanished. The entire party, plus Quetzalcoatl, were on a city street. Not the street near Maria's restaurant. It looked more like downtown.

Éduard turned and saw Bunker Hill, a prominent rocky outcropping that jutted into the city of LA. Cut into it was a tunnel for all the cars that needed to move through the hills that separated downtown from Crown Hill. Another one nearby went the other way.

"The Third Street tunnel?" Éduard asked.

"Yes," Quetzalcoatl said. "Your test is to save one living human who is stuck in his vehicle in the middle of that tunnel."

Éduard thought that wouldn't be too difficult in normal times, even without a car. There was a sidewalk on one side, walking through the tunnel was not difficult. Right at the moment, though, there was one problem. Or perhaps it could be said that there were many problems. A mob of zombies filled the entrance of the tunnel, and more were packed into the tunnel itself, as far as the eye could see.

"They're all trying to eat one human?"

"Indeed." The feathered serpent leaned forward. "If you emerge from the other side of the tunnel, with the human still alive, I will help you."

"Who is the human? Someone important?"

"Humans are never important, except as masses that worship me. This one chose to drive through the tunnel at the wrong time."

"Say, Quetzy," Gary said, floating near the giant snake's head. "We don't have to do this. We don't need you. We'll just get to our meeting some other way."

"Too late," Quetzalcoatl said. He raised himself off the pavement and floated in the air. "You may fly away, ghost, but for your friends there is only one way out, through that tunnel."

Éduard turned to look toward the east, where the street ran between tall buildings. There was no clear path. The monsters who had been introduced earlier stood in a semicircle. Maria wore her skull face. La Cadejo growled, glowing eyes looking particularly evil. El Silbon whistled his musical scales. The others did their best to look threatening.

"There's just a few of them," Larthia said. "We can get past them."

"I eat monsters for breakfast," Lazarko growled. "Or lunch, dinner. Any meal really."

Movement behind the monsters quickly resolved into short figures in straw hats. Hundreds of duendes formed ranks behind La Llorona and showed sharp-toothed grins.

""Maybe not," Éduard said. He turned to face the gaping maw of the Third Street tunnel. "Gary, you won't be hurt by the zombies. How about you scout things out? See what condition the human is in."

"I'm on it." The ghost sailed over the heads of the zombie hordes, disappearing down the tunnel.

"Lazarko, you should wait here. You're the only one they want to eat."

"You calling me coward? I go," the Russian said.

"We're not totally immune," Larthia said. "One of them bit you, dear."

"I'm sure that was a mistake. It didn't realize I wasn't alive."

"They don't seem very bright. Enough mistakes and we'll be torn apart before they can apologize."

"I suppose."

"I don't have all day," Quetzalcoatl said in a godly, amplified voice. "Are you going in there or not?"

"You're immortal, Quetzy," Larthia snapped at the Meso-American god. "You have forever. Chill."

Gary came out of the tunnel. He looked ill. "It's as dark as *Thirty Days of Night* in there. I had to pass through a lot of those things. It was gross."

"What about the human?"

"He's alive, barely. I don't think he's eaten or had water for days. Zombies are piled on top of his car like gay men in the back room of a West Hollywood club."

Wind blew through the tunnel, bringing a stench that was hard to take. "Zombie movies never tell you that they stink," Éduard held his nose closed.

"That's it!"

"That's what, Gary?"

"In *The Walking Dead* they cover themselves in gore and they can walk right past the zombies."

"In *Shaun of the Dead* they just walk like zombies," Éduard said. "They're both fiction, it can't really work."

"It's worth a try."

Gary was right. Éduard walked toward the tunnel entrance. The mob of zombies had their backs to him, they were so intent on getting to the one human inside. A particularly ripe specimen was little more than a skeleton covered in blood and some muscle tissue. There was no logical reason it could even be moving, but it was.

Éduard took the thing by the neck and dragged it back toward his friends. The lower jaw chomped but couldn't get its teeth into the vampire. The chest cavity was filled with a red mass of gore. Éduard pushed his other hand under the ribs and pulled out the liquefying remains of various organs. He spread it all over his 18th century costume. "Everybody take some."

"You are joking," Lazarko said. "This is expensive suit."

"You need it most of all," Éduard said. "You're alive."

Larthia took a large sample of the blood and ooze and spread it all over herself. "I've tried skin creams that smell better," she said.

"What are you doing?" Quetzalcoatl thundered from above. "Stop stalling!"

"Don't tie your feathers in a knot, Q," Éduard said.

The skeletal zombie managed a short moan. This made a few others turn around and notice the vampires and were-wolf. They began to shuffle away from the tunnel.

"Incoming," Gary said from a position about ten feet above the others.

Éduard cracked the skull of the zombie and plunged his hand inside. He pulled out a mess of brain. The thing collapsed, really dead this time.

"Brains, Ed?" Gary asked. "You hungry?"

"Shut up." The brains did not make him want to eat. The general smell of zombies was repulsive to him. He mushed the gray matter on his face. Larthia spread gore over his back and he did the same for her. They both helped Lazarko finish his coat of blood and rot.

The vampires turned as the new zombies arrived. The creatures held out their hands and moaned, then looked blank. Their interest in the three friends was gone. They turned away, their senses no longer telling them a meal was nearby.

"Ready?" Edward looked at his friends.

"Ready." Larthia looked calm, ready for anything.

"This will be fun," Lazarko said.

"You might not like it as much as you hope." Éduard

picked up the werewolf and threw him over his shoulder. "We have to keep you away from them as much as possible."

"Put me down!"

Éduard and Larthia ran toward the tunnel. When they got close to the zombies they used their vampire abilities to make themselves lighter and jumped high. They proceeded into the Third Street tunnel, stepping on heads and pushing off with their feet.

Soon they plunged into utter darkness. Éduard had assumed the normal lights along the sides would be on, but there was no light at all. It did make sense that power would have failed in the week or so since Halloween, when it all started. He really wasn't sure how long it had been.

Straining his vampire senses to the max, Eduard jumped from one zombie head or shoulder to the next, vaulting as far as possible between landing and jumping again. Larthia did the same near him. She was actually better at this sort of thing than he was. She had lived for many centuries before artificial light was invented.

There were a lot of cars, some with zombified drivers and passengers inside, unable to get out. Some had roofs that provided a few sure steps before Éduard had to jump on heads again.

Lazarko made it known that he did not like being carried like a sack of potatoes. He struggled, shifting his weight and making each jump riskier.

The sound of the zombies moaning was amplified by the hard tunnel walls. It became so loud as Éduard jumped through the stygian darkness that he couldn't hear anything else. The smell was concentrated by the closeness of the undead bodies and the still air of the passage under the mountain. The vampire's usual ability to discern scents and follow odor trails was overwhelmed by the smell of rot.

The inevitable happened. Éduard missed a step and his foot fell in a space between zombies. He tumbled forward, Lazarko being tossed ahead of him and his own body hitting hard on a skull that had just a few scraps of scalp on it. He found himself halfway between the heads of the zombie mob and the pavement of the tunnel. The creatures were so tightly packed in the tunnel that he was stuck at about thigh level.

It seemed that the gore Éduard had spread on himself was doing its job. None of his new friends paid any attention to him. Or maybe that was just because he was a vampire. His newfound desire to eat flesh was not triggered in the least by the masses of dead flesh around him.

The biggest test of the gore-spreading theory of zombie avoidance would be Lazarko. He had warm blood and a pumping heart. As a human or a wolf, he should be a dinner bell calling out to the flesh-chompers that surrounded him. Éduard hoped that he was okay.

Clawing his way up, the vampire got his feet on the pavement and did his best to move forward, toward the car where a human needed to be rescued. The only way to make any progress was to move zombies out of his way. He grabbed them and threw them behind him, or shredded them with his claws and left them in pools of blood and ripped flesh that he stepped over.

"You're going the wrong way."

"Gary?"

"You got turned around when you fell."

Éduard turned to his right until Gary said, "That's good."

"Is Lazarko okay?"

"He's holding his own. You're almost to the car."

The vampire pushed his way forward in the direction Gary had showed him. He quickly discovered that keeping himself covered in gore to distract the zombies would not be a problem. Each new body that he displaced provided more blood and viscera, which coated him from head to toe. He stank as much as any zombie, and could easily be mistaken for one.

The first thing he would do if he ever got out of this, Éduard thought, was take a long hot shower.

From above, a cascade of gore fell on the vampire, soaking him even more than he already was. Blood fell on him like a waterfall. It drenched him until there was no part of him, no matter how private, that wasn't slimy with ichor.

That's not the kind of shower I had in mind, Éduard thought.

CHAPTER TWENTY

"SORRY, DARLING," CAME LARTHIA'S VOICE.

Éduard spat blood out. Blood that didn't taste at all appealing. "Did you do that, dear?"

"I moved a couple of zombies on this pile, and all that stuff fell out. Are you all right?"

"Pile?" Éduard felt in front of him and realized that there was a hill of zombies in front of him. He moved his hands up. It went further up than he could reach.

"Can you come up and give me a hand?"

"You're at the car," Gary said. "Larthia's on top, Lazarko's on the other side."

Éduard gripped the clothing of a zombie in front of him, a large lady in a tube top and shorts, and stepped up on another one, a black man in a running outfit. The zombies shifted under him as he pulled himself up. He made himself lighter, but not too much. He could barely see where he was going.

At the top, Larthia said, "We have to get all of them off the car."

"How can we move a human past all these zombies?"

Loud cursing came up the pile. "I hate these guys." Lazarko stood next to the two vampires.

"Coat him in nasty stuff, is the first thing. Gary, is he conscious? Have you told him we're trying to rescue him?"

"Living humans can't hear me."

"Right. How does he seem?"

"He goes in and out. Sometimes he shouts 'We'll fix it in post!'"

"Keep an eye on him."

Gary sank down through the squirming zombie bodies and into the unseen car below. The vampires and the werewolf started tossing undead bodies off the pile and kicking the heads of new ones that tried to climb up.

"Reminds me of the time we posed as French soldiers in the Napoleonic wars, just for fun," Larthia said. "We helped a general when he lost a brooch in a mass grave of his own soldiers."

"Yes, he said his wife gave it to him for good luck on the battlefield."

"And she would kill him if he didn't bring it back."

"We looked in there for days, moving bodies around. Then he found the brooch in his tent."

"He was delicious."

"The upper classes have the tastiest blood."

"Guys, stop reminiscing and get down here." Gary's head popped out of the top of the car, which was now revealed. "We need to get this guy out of here."

With the top of the car cleared, the question arose of how they were going to remove the human from inside. It was a large, expensive SUV. No sun roof, unfortunately.

"We'll have to break a window, get in there and coat him in gore."

"You do that, darling. Lazarko and I will fight off the zombies."

"And pass me plenty of blood and guts."

Larthia leaned forward and planted a bloody kiss on Éduard's lips. "We'll have such stories to tell about all this," she said.

"If we survive it." Éduard stepped down onto the writhing bodies and pushed his way down. He threw some zombies and decapitated a few more with his claws, finally planting his feet on the pavement. Larthia and Lazarko also moved down, clearing a space around the rear window of the SUV. The human lay on the back seat, with Gary hovering over him.

"Ready?" Éduard asked.

"Ready."

The window shattered with one quick, sharp blow of the vampire's fist. Little cubes of safety glass rained down inside the vehicle. The smell of fresh human made its way out of the opening, creating a frenzy in the zombie mob. Éduard pushed himself up and through the window.

Larthia popped the head off one zombie and aimed the resulting arterial spurt of blood into the car. Éduard set to work smearing the liquid on the living body. When the blood flow stopped, Lazarko threw a length of large intestine through the window, which provided both blood and offal to add to the coating of gore.

The human stirred and murmured, "Not a placental mammal."

That should do it, Éduard thought. The human was a tall, slender man with graying hair. He looked vaguely familiar, but there was no time to think about who he was. He was sufficiently covered in zombie scent so the vampire started to pass him, head first, out the window. Lazarko seized the man's shoulders and pulled him out of the car.

"As fast as we can to the other end of the tunnel," Éduard said.

The ghost nodded. He floated up through the top of the car. The vampire went out the window.

"They lost interest in him when you put the stuff on him," Larthia said.

"Then we just have to take him to face Quetzy."

That was easier said than done. The vampires had to leap over the heads of the ravening undead, while the were-wolf bulled his way through with tooth and claw. All of them were so covered in the smelliest, stinkiest, and stickiest byproducts of the human body that it got into their ears and mouths and noses.

Éduard carried the human over his shoulder, but he was lighter than Lazarko, and barely conscious, so he was easier to carry than the werewolf.

The effort was helped a little because the lure of a warm, edible human no longer drew the zombies toward the center of the tunnel and they began to drift away towards both ends, spilling out into the city of Los Angeles to seek other prey.

Éduard became aware of the man's beating heart as he carried him. All he could smell was zombie, but he could feel the blood flowing through the warm body. He began to salivate. The man had plenty of flesh too, even though he was thin. *Once we show him off to the crazy Aztec god,* Éduard thought, *that flesh and blood is mine.* Then he realized he should let Larthia have some blood. She wouldn't want the flesh, though, that was all his. His stomach began to rumble at the thought.

It was still night in the city outside of the tunnel, and the streetlights were out, but there were a few glimpses of light, of car headlights on the roads and stars in the sky, as he got closer to the end.

The zombies were thinning out, leaving the tunnel. The vampire found himself walking on the pavement instead of jumping on heads. He had to shove zombies aside to get through them, but they just moaned and shambled away.

"There you are," Larthia said. She came close and put her arm in Éduard's. "How is our charge?"

"Heart is still beating."

"That is good."

Gary floated up to the vampires. "Did Lazarko make it?"

"Haven't seen him for a while."

The sound of bones cracking came from behind. A fat male zombie wondered past the vampires. He had been ripped in half, with only his spine connecting his hips to his rib cage, the upper half hanging and his head dragging on the ground along with his guts. The weight of his upper half made him topple over, but his legs kept trying to walk.

"That teaches him to try and bite me." Lazarko emerged into what little light there was. He licked blood off his fingers as if he had just consumed a three-piece KFC dinner.

The group emerged from the tunnel and looked around. There was no feathered serpent. There were no monsters and no duendes. It was still night time, so the vampires had no problem standing in the open. Éduard put his human burden on the ground. The man stirred a little but didn't open his eyes.

"He ditched us?" Gary asked. "I've never been ditched by a god before. A couple of guys with the body of Apollo, but no real gods."

"Muy bien, vampiros." Maria sat on a nearby abandoned

car. She jumped to the ground and walked toward Éduard and his party.

"Where's Quetzalcoatl?" Éduard asked.

"He had a thing. He was sure you would never make it through there. I will tell him you survived. He will be at your meeting. If you can get there." She floated up into the air and flew out of sight. The first flicker of dawn showed over the mountain they had just passed through.

"I've completely lost track of what day it is," Eduard said. He pulled his phone out. The battery was very low but he was still able to read the date. "The meeting is tonight."

The vampires and werewolf turned to face a city full of zombies. With daylight coming on, they had to cross miles of urban territory to get to their destination.

"How 'bout a snack?" Éduard picked up the human and prepared to bite his neck.

"You can bite him?" Larthia asked. "With all the zombie stuff all over him?"

It was true that the human did not smell very inviting. "Maybe we can wash him." Éduard looked around. He didn't see anywhere to do that.

"How can you eat?" Lazarko patted his belly. "I am stuffed like it's Maslenitsa."

"You're full of zombie meat and you think of a Russian pancake festival?"

"I have good imagination."

Éduard shook his head. "I would think all that rotting meat would make you sick."

"I have stomach like cast iron," the werewolf replied.

"We'd better get off the streets," Larthia said. She was right, the sun was doing its thing to the east, and they wouldn't be in shade for long.

A sign that said Flower Street faced the exit from the

tunnel. There was a tall building to the left, some trees in the area, and a big apartment or condo building a little further down. The tall building looked like the best bet.

At street level an entrance to a garage was the obvious way to enter, but zombies could be inside. Éduard entered carefully, carrying the unconscious human. He found a door that led to a stairway.

Lazarko went through the door, and reported that the stairway was clear. They went up to the lobby level of the building.

Bathrooms presented themselves and Éduard carried the human into the men's room. Larthia entered right behind him, and Gary entered through the wall. Lazarko came in a moment later and went straight into a booth, closing the door. There was no light in there but the vampires could see pretty well.

Éduard took a handful of paper towels. Luckily, the water still worked, and he soaked the towels until they dripped all over the place. He rubbed the human's face to get zombie blood off it. The man fluttered his eyelids and said, "How deep is the Lusitania?"

"I wouldn't mind getting a bath too," Éduard said. "Or at least a shower."

"I know," Larthia said. "I feel sticky all over."

"All this blood and gore makes me wonder something."

"What's that, dear?"

"In movies, one bite turns humans into zombies. Unless they cut off the arm or leg where the bite is."

"So?"

"So why doesn't getting zombie blood on you make you a zombie? Some has to go in your mouth, or in wounds. If it's a virus, it would transmit that way as well as a bite." Éduard took some more paper towel and wetted it. He tried to clean all of the man's visible skin.

"I guess because they're movies, dear. Sometimes you just have to accept the conventions."

"I suppose. I wish I could think of a logical reason. Well, this guy is as clean as I can make him here." He raised the human toward his mouth. "Do you want any?"

"Wait."

Éduard paused. "What?"

"I'm not sure in this light. Can you take him out where we can see him better?"

"You're delaying my snacking, but all right."

In the hallway, there was enough light to see by, but not enough to make the vampires uncomfortable. Gary was out there, floating. "Finished?" he asked.

"Hold him up," Larthia said. Eduard adjusted his grip on the human and lifted his head up.

"I think that's..."

Gary floated closer, then gasped when he saw the man's face.

"John Carnahan," Larthia and Gary said at the same time.

CHAPTER TWENTY-ONE

"Really?" Éduard asked. The man's hair was still matted with blood so it was hard to match his face with the one on TV interviews.

"I'm sure, darling. Remember I talked to him in person once."

"I'm torn between asking him for juicy behind the scenes details about his films and drinking his blood until he's deader than we are."

"I'm hungry too," Larthia said, "but I think we should talk to him first."

Éduard placed the director on the floor of the hallway. "I haven't had fresh human blood for days. I don't know if I can control myself."

"I want to ask him if he ever saw Arnim Blackenovum naked," Gary said. He had a dreamy look in his eye. "I would have done anything to see that when he was in his prime. I even loved the cute accent."

The door of the bathroom opened and Lazarko came out. He looked pale. "You were right, zombie flesh not so good for tummy." He saw the human lying on the floor. "What, you haven't sucked him dry yet?"

"It's John Carnahan," Larthia said. "Director of *The Dominator* and *Lusitania.*"

"So? Movie directors don't taste good to vampires?"

"Larthia thinks we should talk to him."

"Never talk to people in the show business," Lazarko said. "All jerks, believe me."

Carnahan stirred and moaned, then put his hand on his head.

"All right," Éduard said. "Talk to him, but he is going to be my next meal."

The director sat up. "Where am I?" He looked up. "Who are you?"

"See? Cliché dialogue," Éduard said. "And he thinks he can write all his own scripts."

"My name is Larthia. This is Éduard and Lazarko."

"Do you have any water?"

Larthia shot Éduard a look. He rolled his eyes but went back into the bathroom. There was nothing in there that resembled a cup, so the vampire put his hands together and ran water into them. He went back into the hall, walking carefully to avoid spilling the water.

"Open."

Carnahan looked startled, but opened his mouth. Éduard poured the water in. "I should be the one drinking."

The director swallowed. "Thanks. Do you have any whiskey? Or food?" His voice was hoarse. "I was trapped in my car for days. How did I get out?"

"We'll explain, Mr. Carnahan," Larthia said, "but if you can walk, we could go look for some food."

"Sure. I think." Carnahan weakly tried to stand, until

Lazarko grabbed him by the shoulders and lifted him to his feet. "Thanks. No autographs."

"I'll find something." Gary vanished down the hall.

"Thanks, Gary," Éduard said.

"Who's Gary?" Carnahan asked.

"A ghost we know."

The famous director shook his head. "My ears must be bad. I thought you said he's a ghost."

"That's right," Larthia said. "And we're vampires." She indicated herself and Éduard. "He's a werewolf."

"Is this a pitch? You guys have a script? I don't do woo-woo shit. Talk to Spielberg."

Lazarko stood in front of Carnahan and flashed into werewolf form. He let out a fearsome growl.

"That's good work. Who did it? Rick Baker? Rob Bottin? I'd say Stan Winston, but he's dead."

"We are really vampires and a werewolf. I'm Larthia, this is Eduard, and that's Lazarko."

"All right. I'm game. There's a real zombie apocalypse going on, so why not vamps and werewolves?"

Gary came through a wall and pointed. "There's a small restaurant in the lobby."

"Gary found a restaurant, Mr. Carnahan," Larthia said.

"Great. I could eat a grimhorse. "

Everyone looked blank. "The animals they ride in *Examplar*? Don't you people go to the movies?"

"We have a home theater," Éduard said. "I collect many different types of home video."

"You have to see *Examplar* in 3D IMAX, Ed. The sequels will be even better."

The group followed the ghost down the hall and emerged in a large open area. Along one wall was a building directory and a security guard's desk, with no security guard visible.

A bank of elevators was nearby. Another wall had a sandwich shop. Several small round tables, with ice-cream-parlor chairs, were in front of it.

Someone moaned. Éduard saw the security guard stand up behind the desk. His uniform was red with blood that dripped from a flap of scalp, complete with ear, that bounced up and down as he moved. The zombie bumped into the waist-high door of the security booth, turned around, and walked slowly the other way.

"I'll kill it," Lazarko said.

"Leave him," Carnahan said. "He's too stupid to get out of there. Reminds me of the head of script development at Fox."

Larthia was the first to catch the smell as they walked into the restaurant. It was just a counter with a kitchen behind it, and an area for customers to order. The smell came from a selection of pre-made sandwiches in plastic containers. The plastic was green with mold. A couple had burst open.

"Power's been out for a while," Éduard said. Is there anything a human can eat?"

Larthia opened the refrigerator and made a disgusted face. "There's water, though it's warm." She took a bottle and closed the door. Then she opened a cabinet door under the counter. "Here's something," she said. She pulled out a large industrial sized can that was marked CHILI. She put the can next to the sink.

"Why exactly are we feeding him instead of eating him?" Éduard asked.

"Maybe he can help. He can drive a car, get us to the Tar Pits."

"Lazarko could do that."

"All right, I want to ask him something that has always bugged me," Larthia said.

"What?"

"*The Dominator* is a grandfather paradox."

"You mean you can't go back in time and kill your grandfather, because then you wouldn't be born?"

"Yes. If the Dominator succeeded in killing the lady, there would be no reason to send him back in time."

"He didn't succeed."

"But that was what the machine wanted. The mission could not succeed, it cancels itself out."

"For that you're going to give up a nice meal of blood? When we've had so little recently?" Éduard asked.

"We can suck him dry after I ask the question. And I doubt he will answer unless we feed him first."

"All right. How are you going to open that can?" Éduard pointed to the electric can opener on the counter. "No power."

Larthia smiled and extended her vampire claws. She ripped the top off the can, leaving the metal jagged. Cheap chili spilled on the counter and the floor.

"That's why I love you," Éduard said. "You can't heat it up though."

"I don't think he'll be too fussy." Larthia poured some of the chili in a bowl and found a large spoon. She carried it out to the tables in front of the restaurant.

Gary wasn't in the area. Maybe he went out scouting, Éduard thought.

John Carnahan sat at one of the tables, with Lazarko in a chair opposite him. "So a silver bullet would work," he said.

Lazarko said, "I have never been shot by one, but they tell me it works."

"I had an argument with a friend when I was a kid," the director said. "He said if werewolves can only be killed by a silver bullet, they never die of disease or old age."

"No no, we get old, like all peoples. Though I have never been really sick."

Larthia put the cold chili and the warm water on the table. "Don't eat too fast, Mr. Carnahan."

Carnahan took one look at the chili and took a big spoonful. He put it all in his mouth and chewed. "This is terrible." He took more from the bowl. "But great. Oh god, I thought I would never eat again." He unscrewed the top of the water bottle and guzzled the contents.

He finished the bowl in a few more bites, then looked at Lazarko. "But you have werewolves in the family. Do you know some that died of old age?" He looked strange, turned and vomited chili and water all over the floor of the lobby.

"I warned you," Larthia said.

"Can I get some more?" Carnahan asked.

"I'm a several thousand-year-old vampire, I have seduced and killed kings and titans of industry. I have performed evil that would make your mind run screaming into the infinite depths of insanity. I am not a waitress."

"I'll get it," Éduard said. "Just don't make her any madder while I'm gone." He went into the restaurant and got the can of chili. He brought it out and poured a small amount into the bowl.

"Incredible," Carnahan said. "There are really vampires. And I never liked vampire movies."

"My favorite movie of yours, John, was *The Really Really Deep Place*."

"Yeah? That shoot was hard. Weeks of diving in huge tanks. Not as hard as *Lusitania*, though. Water is a bitch to shoot in."

"Eat your chili, John," he emphasized the name and looked at Larthia. "Then we have to decide what to do with you."

"Whether you're going to suck my blood or not?"

"Did Larthia tell you?"

"No, just makes sense. That's what vamps do, and I'm just about the only fresh, un-zombified human around."

The zombie guard moaned. His arms were outstretched toward the party at the tables, but he still couldn't get out of his booth.

"Well, yeah," Éduard said. "Your blood smells very good from here." And your flesh, he thought. He fought down the zombie desire. If it took over he might never be himself again.

"So what are two vampires, a werewolf, and a ghost doing walking around in a zombie apocalypse? If you walked into a bar, I would at least expect a good punchline."

Larthia sat at the table. "Well, it's a bit of a story."

"Stories are my business."

Larthia told Carnahan everything from the start, the fated Halloween evening when the Santa Monica street festival was interrupted by real zombies. Éduard listened. Lazarko sat in another chair and dozed off.

"Now that's a movie," Carnahan said at the end. "I would pitch that to Universal in a heartbeat. They're all about monsters."

"We're not monsters," Éduard objected. "I like to think of us as useful predators. We cull the weak from the herd."

"Monsters sell tickets, Ed. You could be a rich vampire."

"Keep talking."

"Needs an ending," Carnahan said. "You're meeting at the Tar Pits could end the second act, but it needs something bigger for the climax."

"Do you have something in mind?" Larthia asked.

"If you don't eat me, I'll help you get to the Tar Pits, and then I might know someone who could help end the zombie apocalypse."

"Really?" Éduard asked. He had started to think the quest was foolish and they would accomplish nothing. "Who?"

"I'd rather not say, yet. I don't want to get your hopes up."

"Where do we find this person?" Larthia asked.

"That's the tough part," the director said. "First we have to get to my submarine."

CHAPTER TWENTY-TWO

BEFORE ÉDUARD COULD ASK CARNAHAN ABOUT HIS submarine, Gary floated up to the group. "I found a truck with keys in it. Éduard and Larthia can stay in the back, with the back door closed. The only trouble is, it's locked."

"Who are you all looking at?" Carnahan said. "Must be Gary. Hi, Gary!" He waved in the wrong direction.

"Hi, John," Gary said. "By the way, *False Truths* sucked. Blackenovum as an American spy? With that accent? Does the CIA recruit in Austria?"

The two vampires laughed. "What?" Carnahan asked. "Did he say something about me?"

"No, he found a truck we can use," Éduard said. "But we have to break into it."

"I see, without breaking a window so the zoms can't get in."

"I didn't think of that."

"You have to think of the dramatic possibilities in every situation. And the challenges the heroes face."

"Everything is about movies to you, isn't it?"

"Life is about movies, Ed. Let's take a look at that truck."

Carnahan stood up. "Gary? Lead the way!"

"How?" Gary asked. "He can't see or hear me."

"Go with Gary, Lazarko. John will follow you."

The ghost, the werewolf, and the director left the lobby. Éduard and Larthia sat at one of the little tables. The zombie guard moaned and stumbled back and forth in the security booth.

"I wonder how they're going to get into that truck," Larthia said after a while.

"If this was a movie, it would show them figuring it out."

"Maybe it will be a movie someday. About the heroic vampires who saved the world."

Éduard shook his head. "Even if we succeed, I don't think anyone will ever believe the story. It's too far-fetched."

"Someone could write a book."

"Sure. A self-published horror comedy that no one will read. By an author who for some reason chose me as the point of view character, so he or she can't show the more interesting stuff going on at the truck."

"Now you're being silly," Larthia said.

"That's me, vampirus ridiculus."

The vampires fell into a spell of quietly thinking for a good twenty minutes, until a huge crash and tinkle of breaking glass came from another part of the building. Éduard and Larthia jumped up and ran to see what had caused the commotion.

A large delivery truck, featuring a pig standing on its hind legs and wearing a chef's hat, while holding a spatula, and the words "Peter's Pork Products – You'll Squeal with Delight!" on the side, had backed through a glass wall, leaving large shards of glass all over the floor.

"My idea!" Gary said, coming out the sliding back door

of the truck. "There's enough shade inside here that you guys can get in the truck and ride in the back."

"Thanks, I guess," Éduard said.

Lazarko came from the cab of the truck, his expensive shoes crunching on glass. He undid the latch on the door of the truck and pushed the door up. "Here you go."

A wave of rotting meat smell came out of the dark confines of the cargo area of the truck. The vampires stepped back and Lazarko put his hand over his nose.

John Carnahan jumped down from the driver's seat and came to the back. "What's the awful – " He looked at the truck and the boxes inside, all with the pig cook and slogan on them. "Refrigeration not working for over a week, huh?"

"With our senses, how can we ride in there?" Éduard asked Larthia.

"We survived riding in a train full of cattle from Abilene to Chicago. What year was that?"

"1873. The cattle were alive. It was their dung that stank the place up."

"Hey, no problem." Lazarko stepped on the truck's bumper and entered the back. Soon boxes of rotting pork sausages and chops came flying out of the darkness, landing on the floor of the building with a squishy thud.

"There!" The werewolf said when he was done. He jumped to the floor and stood next to Éduard.

"It's still going to stink in there."

"You folks don't have much choice," Carnahan said. "It's this or stay here and miss your meeting."

"It will be fine." With her usual grace, Larthia vampire-floated into the truck. Éduard shrugged and followed her.

"You sure we can trust the human?" he asked. "We could just suck him dry and Lazarko could drive."

"He did say he might know someone who can help us."

"He probably said that so we wouldn't suck him dry."

"Give him a chance, dear."

"Have nice trip," Lazarko said. He pulled the door of the truck down and total darkness took over.

"He didn't leave us anywhere to sit," Éduard complained.

Soon the engine rumbled to life and the truck began to move. Éduard sat with his back against one wall. The smell was still very bad. Larthia sat next to him. "We haven't slept since we were at the pixie building."

Éduard didn't think it was a good idea to go inert and not be aware of danger, but the sound of the engine, the motion of the truck, and soothing motion as the large vehicle rolled over large bumps, presumably zombies, sent him into vampire slumber.

The truck door rattled open. Éduard stood, ready to rip an intruder apart with his vampire claws. Lazarko smiled at him. "Wakey wakey! We're here!"

It was still sunny out, but the truck was parked with its rear in shade. The two vampires looked out and saw carefully manicured trees and a broad lawn, with the wall of a house next to the truck. Overhead a roof stretched between the house and a garage. Éduard stepped down and was joined by Larthia on a gravel driveway. "We're where?" he asked.

"Carnahan's house. Malibu."

"I thought he was taking us to the Tar Pits."

"First things first," John Carnahan said, walking from bright sunlight into the shade. "You want to make your pitch looking like you just came off a shift in a slaughterhouse?"

Éduard had become so used to being covered in gore he hadn't given a thought to how it would look at the meeting. His Anne Rice vampire suit was a red mess plastered to his skin, and Larthia, Lazarko and Carnahan also looked like extras in the lawnmower scene in *Dead Alive*.

"We have plenty of time to make your meeting," Carnahan said, moving to a door that lead into the house. "If vampires and werewolves take showers, you're welcome to do it in here."

It would be nice to get the sticky feeling off, Éduard realized. He looked at Larthia. She nodded.

The door let them into an enormous kitchen with more islands than the Bahamas. Carnahan showed them five bedrooms, each with a bathroom big enough to hold a reunion meeting of the cast of *Dark Shadows*, living and dead.

"You have power," Éduard said, turning on a floor lamp.

"Generators, and enough diesel to choke a Peterbilt factory."

Lazarko chose a bathroom for himself and the vampires selected one to share. Éduard started to fill a bathtub that was almost a small swimming pool. He took his costume off, having to peel some it off by force. Gobbets of flesh fell out of it and plopped on the tile floor.

Between his clothing and Larthia's, the pile on the floor looked like the aftermath of a productive day for John Wayne Gacy and Ted Bundy working together.

As soon as the two vampires stepped into the water, it turned a deep pink. Then it became red as they scrubbed each other with loofahs they found next to the tub.

"There you are," Gary said. His ghostly body poked out of the wall next to the medicine cabinet. "I got lost, this house is huge."

"We're a little busy, Gary," Éduard said.

"Right, of course. Later." The ghost vanished back into the wall.

"Nice of Mr. Carnahan to let us use his house," Larthia said.

"Yeah. I'm almost glad I didn't eat him." Impulsively, Éduard planted a kiss on his lover's lips. "Besides bathing, there's something else we haven't done in over a week."

Larthia kissed him back. "Not here, the tub looks like Dexter's breakfast."

Naked, clean, and dripping, the vampires entered the bedroom and fell onto the big soft bed, where they proved how lively the undead can be. Afterward, they lay on their backs and looked at the high ceiling.

"What time is it?" Éduard finally asked.

"I don't know."

"Do we trust Carnahan to get us to the meeting?"

"Of course you do," the movie director said. He had come in without making a sound, but Éduard smelled his blood and flesh. His vampire and zombie desires were triggered by the human.

Carnahan wore a black open collar shirt with black jeans, and a black sportscoat. Bright white tennis shoes provided quite a contrast. "I want to see the third act of this story. And if we do stop the zombie apocalypse, I want exclusive rights. It'll be a blockbuster. There's lots of clothing in the closets. Let's go." He turned and left the room.

There were two closets, one with men's clothing and one with women's. Éduard came out of his closet looking like a shorter clone of Carnahan. The sleeves of the jacket he chose were a little too long. Larthia emerged from hers wearing a white blouse, a red knee-length skirt, and black high-heeled shoes.

"You look great," Éduard said. "There are two full length mirrors in there. I wish I could see myself in them."

"We're each other's mirrors," Larthia said. "You look like him."

"I know, everything he has is like this. And there are a hundred of pairs of white tennis shoes."

"You're lucky, the only shoes I could find have these heels. Why humans wear such ridiculous things I will never understand."

"You have worn corsets, hoop skirts, and bustles over the centuries. High heels are not that bad," Éduard said.

"And you looked grand in a powdered wig, or a tall silk hat. Women can't claim the only sartorial silliness."

Éduard bowed. "You are correct as always, my dear. Shall we join the others?"

Like Gary, they got lost trying to find the others. They passed a bowling alley, a video game room, a gym, and a home theater that could hold a Hollywood premiere.

"Here's something," Éduard said. He opened a door that lead outside. The sun was low and the side of the house was shaded. He and Larthia walked out and found a large pool. Outdoor chairs and tables were turned over and one table was smashed.

"What happened?" Larthia asked.

"I don't know," Éduard said, but a moment later, he did know. "The water..."

The water in the pool was churning, waves slapping the sides. When the vampires got closer they saw arms and legs stick up, then sink down. Bodies writhed.

"It's full of zombies," Larthia said. Clearly the sight bothered even her, ancient vampire though she was.

Full of zombies was correct. There wasn't a clear patch of water in the whole pool. Bodies in every possible state of decomposition turned and twisted, collided with each other, grabbed and let go. Jaws opened and closed, arms and legs of some of the zombies passed through the rib cages of others, making a giant jigsaw puzzle of human body parts. A few were just heads that had been severed, rolling in the water, eyes moving, mouths moaning silently. A stench rolled off the pool as well, making it even less inviting for a nice swim.

"Gross, huh?" Carnahan said from behind Éduard. Both vampires jumped, for the first time in their vampiric lives scared by a mere human.

CHAPTER TWENTY-THREE

"D ON'T SNEAK UP ON US LIKE THAT, CARNAHAN," Éduard said.

"Sorry, I didn't know a human could sneak up on a vampire."

"It must be the stench from the pool, it hid your smell."

"What happened here?" Larthia asked. How did all of them get in the pool?"

"You will have to ask my wife," the movie director said. "My ex-wife, that is. Come in the living room and she'll tell you."

The room that Carnahan called the living room could accommodate a Super Bowl marching band, though they would have tripped over the many couches and coffee tables, messing up their performance quite a bit. He walked straight toward a flat screen TV mounted on the wall that was bigger than the screen in some movie theaters.

A woman was on the screen, blond and wearing a bathrobe. She had a bottle that looked like vodka in one hand. She looked familiar to Éduard. "Where did you go, John?" she asked. "I was telling you this is my house per the settlement, and you have to get out. I have called my lawyer and he will slap an injunction on you so fast that your head will spin."

"I was just finding the guests. We'll be leaving soon," Carnahan said.

Éduard realized that the woman was Lisa Burr, the star of "The Dominator," and "Dominator 2," who played the woman that the machine from the future wanted to kill. "Hi," he said. "I'm a big fan of the Dominator movies. Except the crappy recent ones."

"Who the fuck cares?" the woman asked. "I'm talking to John."

"Why is your ex-wife on your TV?" Larthia asked.

"She's in the panic suite," Carnahan said. "When I bought this house I put a whole secure apartment underneath so we could survive anything from storms, fires, civil collapse, or even a complete republican takeover of the federal government."

"And now I get to enjoy it all alone, 'cause this is my house," Burr said. "There's enough food, booze, movies, and porn in here to last years." She turned away and coughed.

"Before we go, please tell me how the pool became full of zombies."

"If you promise to go right after."

"Of course," Carnahan said.

"They broke the gate down when I was sunbathing," Burr said. "I couldn't get to the panic suite door. So I jumped in the pool."

"That didn't keep them away?" Larthia asked.

"For a while. They stood at the edge staring at me and moaning. Then one fell in and the rest followed, like have you seen penguins in nature shows? When they go in the water they all go at once." The movie actress coughed twice. Her face started to look haggard.

"Tell them how you got out," Carnahan said.

"There were so many I was able to walk on them. Then I ran and got in here." She lifted the bottle and gulped a large amount of booze. "I got a scratch somehow." She leaned over and rubbed her leg.

"So sorry to hear that. Well, we'll be off, I hope you have fun in there."

"More than you," Burr said. "I hope the zombies get you."

"I'm doing surprisingly well," the director said. "And are you sure that's just a scratch?"

"Why? I didn't get bit, I'm sure." Her face started to look worse. Veins were clear beneath her skin.

"Completely sure?"

"Sure I'm sure. I --" Lisa Burr looked confused for a second, then her mouth dropped open and drool dripped out. She began to moan.

"I had to see that," Carnahan said. "I bet I can get the house back now."

CHAPTER TWENTY-FOUR

"Sunset is coming on, Mr. Carnahan," Éduard said. "How are we getting down to the Tar Pits?"

"Follow me." The movie director left the room.

Éduard gave Larthia a look. She shrugged. They followed Carnahan. He led them through the house to a small room lined with bookshelves. Several big comfortable leather armchairs dotted the room, each with a reading lamp behind it.

Lazarko slept in one of the chairs, snoring loudly. He woke with a snort when Carnahan and the vampires entered. "What? About time. Carny man tell me to meet him here an hour ago."

"Do you read a lot?" Larthia asked Carnahan. "You seem like a very busy man, without much spare time for reading."

"True," the director said, "But books tell stories in the best way. Inside your head. They beat movies, TV, virtual reality, everything. And a few books in here are relevant to our situation."

"Really?" Éduard asked. "Which ones?"

Carnahan moved to one of the shelves. "This is my

horror section. I have every known vampire book, from *The Vampyr* to *Varney the Vampire* to *Carmilla*. And of course, *Dracula.*"

"You should meet him. Full of himself, not that interesting."

"Meet Dracula? You're kidding."

"No."

"If we get out of this zombie thing, I'm going to insist on meeting him. If you like something more modern and with some humor, try *Bite Club* by Hal Bodner."

"Éduard has a very large movie collection," Larthia said. "He doesn't read much."

"I read that, what was it?"

"*Salem's Lot*?"

"Yeah, that was pretty good."

"I have a whole Stephen King section, if you ever care to peruse it." Carnahan pointed to another shelf. "Here are zombie books, from *World War Z* to *Patient Zero* to *The Reapers*. And of course the plague series, *Plague Town, Plague Nation,* and *Plague World,* by Dana Fredsti. Not to mention *The Hungry* series by Booth and Shannon."

"Don't we have a meeting to get to?" Larthia asked.

"Of course," Carnahan said. He walked to a small bust of Shakespeare that sat on one table. He pushed the bard's head back to reveal a red button. "This makes me feel very Batman," he said. He pushed the button.

A section of bookcases moved back behind the others, and slid to the side. The director gestured to everyone to walk through the opening. The vampires and the werewolf entered. Once inside a small enclosed area, a door closed. Carnahan opened a panel and pushed another button. The enclosure began to rise.

"It's an elevator," Lazarko said, stating the obvious.

The smell of fresh blood and meat that came from Carnahan made Éduard drool.

They didn't travel far. The door opened and a fresh breeze that smelled of the ocean swirled around everyone.

"There you are," a voice said. It was Gary. "I've been waiting here on the roof for a long time."

Carnahan produced two large blankets from somewhere. "You'll have to make a dash for it under these." He handed one each to Éduard and Larthia.

"Where are we going?" Larthia asked.

"You'll see. Come on."

The vampires wrapped the blankets around themselves and walked out onto the roof of the fabulous estate. "Is helicopter," Lazarko said. "We fly to Tar Pits!"

"I wish you guys could see this sunset," Gary said. "The ocean is right there. I'd die for a house around here. I mean, even deader than I already am."

"Sunset is for tourists," Lazarko said.

After being guided up a few steps into the helicopter, Éduard and Larthia were able to unwrap themselves. They could see that there was still light outside, but the back of the aircraft was dark.

"Put the headphones and seatbelts on," Carnahan said as he settled in the pilot's seat. Lazarko sat in a seat next to him.

The engines started up, making a lot of noise. Éduard put on the headset next to his seat and the sound was reduced to a low background sound. He also attached his seatbelt. He felt the fairy jar in his pocket.

He saw that Larthia put her headphone and seatbelt on too, as did Lazarko.

Gary poked his head in. I'm going to have to fly on my own, as usual. See you there." Then he was gone.

The helicopter lifted into the air. Éduard's stomach lurched. He still didn't quite trust modern flying machines. To have something else to think about, he took the jar out of his pocket.

"I still have this. I wasn't sure if I should bring it."

The fairy queen looked out though the glass for a second, then disappeared in a swirl.

"Maybe someone at the meeting can open it."

"Worth a try." Éduard put the jar back in his pocket.

"Welcome to Carnahan Airways," the director said through the headphones. "I'll have you at the La Brea Tar Pits in a jiffy."

"Is all burning," Lazarko said.

"What's all burning?" Éduard asked.

"Whole city."

Éduard was afraid that made sense. Without the efforts of the fire crews that suppressed every wild fire, dropping water from helicopters and battling the flames with shovels and determination, Los Angeles was a conflagration waiting to happen. He couldn't see the ground, but the sky was full of smoke.

"As long as we have a few minutes, let me ask," Carnahan said. "What's your pitch?"

Éduard adjusted the little microphone that was attached to his headphones. "Pitch?"

"Your angle, what you're going to say to convince the crowd to help you."

Éduard looked at Larthia. She spoke into her mike. "We'll just talk to them," she said.

"You gotta have an angle, folks. Something that appeals to them. Make them like you, make them want to help."

"Um...do you have any ideas?" Éduard asked.

"After you get them on your side, tell 'em your plan, how

you're going to end the zombie apocalypse."

Éduard paused for a moment. "I don't know."

"You're going to meeting without a pitch? It'll never work. Okay, what caused the zombie plague?"

"Is virus, right?" Lazarko asked.

"In some movies," Éduard said. "But in *Night of the Living Dead* it was mysterious radiation that came to earth with a satellite that crashed."

"In *Return of the Living Dead,*" Larthia said, "it was from mysterious government barrels that held zombie bodies in liquid."

"Stephen King's *Cell* has a signal coming through cell phones."

"*Pontypool* shows zombieism being transmitted through the English language."

"Okay, okay," Carnahan said. "So no one knows, is what you're telling me."

"Pretty much," Éduard said.

"Then how the fuck do you think you can stop it?"

"We hoped someone at the meeting would have an idea."

"This should be interesting," Carnahan said. The rest of the flight was quiet, except for the sound of the helicopter. The sun went down as they flew, before long the sky was dark and the smoking ruin that was much of Los Angeles was hidden.

"It's weird to see it so dark," Carnahan said. "I used to love the view from Griffith Park of the lights in the LA valley. According to the GPS, we should be over the Tar Pits in a minute."

The GPS satellites didn't lie, the helicopter soon hovered over the site where so many prehistoric animals got stuck in oily muck and died.

"A tourist trap where people go to see animals that were trapped," Éduard mused.

The area was dark, with no sign of any life forms, living or dead, on the ground. The helicopter flew over the museum to the large open space with several clusters of palm trees. It landed and Carnahan cut the engines. "I don't see anybody," he said.

The vampires and the werewolf opened their doors and jumped down to the pavement. Lights that usually bathed the area at night were out. "Maybe no one got the message," Éduard said.

"I sent it before the zombies attacked the pixie building."

Everyone turned toward the voice. "Gary?" Larthia asked.

"I've been behind you the whole way, flying my transparent ass off." The ghost looked around. "Where's the party?"

Carnahan came around the helicopter. "Who are you talking to?"

"Gary's here," Éduard said. "What do you mean party, Gary?"

"I thought more people might come if I hyped it a little."

A single fairy flew from somewhere, circled the group, stopping right next to Éduard's face. "It's them, everyone!" the fairy shouted, in a tiny fairy voice.

In the next moment, the area in front of the Tar Pits museum was flooded with an eerie, soft light. Everyone was there, as if they had been there all along. Fairies, ghosts of humans and animals, including mammoths, saber tooth cats, and direwolves, plus vampires, some of whom Éduard recognized from the vampire bar in West Hollywood, duendes, La Llorona with her monsters, werewolves, and many things that Éduard didn't have a name for. A fairy, probably the same one as before, flew up to Éduard. "You've been brought into the fairy world. Where is the free food and booze?"

The museum was overgrown with plants, and nearby, the tall fence around the tar pits themselves, put there to keep tourists from joining the thousands of deceased animals who didn't look where they were walking, was festooned with vines. Flowers were everywhere and insects buzzed around them.

"Food and booze?" Éduard asked.

"That's what I meant by hyping it a little," Gary said.

"Gary – what did you do?" Éduard asked.

"The post I put on Faebook said it was a party," Gary said. "I didn't think anyone would come to a boring meeting."

"This is amazing," Carnahan said. "Are those fairies? And is that a chupacabra?"

"There's a lot more," Larthia said to Carnahan. "You can't see the ghosts."

"I have to put this scene in the movie," Carnahan said. "The CGI budget will be through the roof, but hell, *Examplar* is pretty much a Pixar film."

"What is THIS?" a fairy asked, hovering near Carnahan.

"A human, but we wouldn't be here without his help," Larthia said.

"You brought a mortal into the fairy world?" The tiny figure said in a shocked voice. "And where is the food and booze?"

"This is an important meeting," Éduard told her. "Not a party."

Something caught the fairy's attention. She turned to look at some new arrivals. "No," she said. "It's a war."

CHAPTER TWENTY-FIVE

A NUMBER OF MINIATURE VEHICLES DROVE THROUGH the crowd, weaving around the legs of solid creatures and through the legs of ghostly ones.

"Pixies!" all the fairies shouted in unison. "Pixies! Pixies! Pixies!" They flew around in circles.

The tiny cars and trucks stopped at the feet of the two vampires. In the lead was the replica of a Porsche Cayenne that had been in Pixie headquarters. The door opened and Anthony Oak stepped out.

"What do we have here?" Carnahan leaned over and stared at the pixie. "He's so cute!"

"Anthony Oak, meet John Carnahan," Éduard said.

"The movie director? I love your documentary about deep ocean diving, Mr. Carnahan."

Carnahan grinned. "Really? Most people don't mention that one. I'd shake your hand, but I might crush you."

"Lift me and Susan up, Éduard," Oak said. The vampire picked them up and held one in each hand. "It's all right, I'm used to dealing with humans," he said to Carnahan. "Verbal exchanges will suffice."

"This is so cool," Carnahan said. "All those monsters and things, fairies and pixies. And ghosts, even though I can't see them."

"Excuse me," a fairy said. She hovered next to Éduard's hand and glared at Anthony. "You are our enemy and we must go to war because you dared come here."

"War?" Anthony looked surprised. "I know we're rivals in many ways, but what makes you want war?"

"You know very well! You trapped our queen in a jar and sold her to a necromancer!"

"Jar?" Oak turned to look at Éduard. "The one you showed me? Do you still have it?"

"It's in my pocket," the vampire said. "I, uh, can't reach for it right now, I have a pixie in each hand."

"Put us together."

Éduard put his hands together, and Oak jumped from the right to the left to join Branch. With one hand free, Éduard reached in his pocket and pulled out the jar. The queen swirled so hard inside that the jar vibrated. "I even asked Quetzalcoatl if he could open it. No dice."

"Can you put me next to it?" Anthony asked.

Éduard put his hands together again. Oak leaned over and knocked on the jar. Everyone else leaned or flew in close to see what was happening.

"This is a great scene," Carnahan said. "Pathos, war, magic, it has everything."

"Poor dear," Larthia said, "I hope we can get her out of there."

The queen stopped swirling for just a second and stared into Anthony's face. Then she blurred again, going round and round very fast.

"I'm sorry," the pixie said. "I have no idea how she got in there. Or how to open it."

"She said she was going to meet with the pixies for peace talks," the fairy squeaked. "We didn't see her again until this guy," she pointed at Éduard, "showed us the jar."

"Peace talks?" Oak frowned. "I never heard of any peace talks. Who would set up peace talks without telling the rest of us. No pixie is that stupid."

Another pixie vehicle, a long limousine, drove up to where everyone was talking. It stopped and a rear door opened.

"Oh no," Anthony Oak said. "Not him. Please."

King Chestnut stepped out of the limo. He strode self-importantly toward Éduard's feet.

"Him!" the fairy flying near Éduard's head shouted. "He's the one the queen was meeting with!"

"Can someone pick up the king?," Oak asked. Éduard looked at Larthia.

"Me? I don't want to touch that guy."

"Please, dear, so we can all talk at the same level."

Fairies flew around the vampire couple, their wings creating an angry buzzing. The rest of the creatures and ghosts had backed off and were watching the drama play out.

King Stump stepped onto Larthia's hand when she bent over. "Nice," he said. "You know you're very attractive for your age." She clearly wanted to squash him but managed to control herself.

"Your Majesty," Anthony Oak said when the king arrived at a similar height. "The fairies seem to think that their queen met with you before she disappeared."

"She met with me? Never. I met with her."

"Then you do know what happened to her?"

"I know what everyone knows, which is that no one

knows. What's true is what's not true, and I know that for sure."

Anthony Oak put his hand over his face and sighed. The fairies flew even faster around the vampires and the pixies they held in their hands.

Carnahan, from outside the circle, pulled out a phone and started to record video of the scene. "Great stuff," he said.

"Sir," Oak said, "the fairies want to go to war over this. We need to find out how their queen ended up inside that jar."

"Oh, that," King Chestnut said. "Some Chinese guy gave me a billion dollars to lure her to a secret meeting and help him trap her in there."

Larthia made a disgusted noise and almost dropped the king. The fairies all stopped in midair and stared at him.

"WHAT?" Oak shouted. "How could you trap the fairy queen in a jar for money?"

"I never did that," Chestnut replied. "Who said I did that?"

"You did! Just now!"

"Wu Keung didn't look like he had a billion dollars," Éduard said.

"I said a million," the king said. "Except I didn't say anything about that, whatever it was."

"Can I throw him in the tar pit?" Larthia asked.

"Did the Chinese guy say anything about how to get her out of there?" Anthony asked.

"No. Not at all. He didn't say that only he had the power to release her. Because I never talked to him."

"Can we find him? Where did you meet him, Éduard? Maybe we can get him here."

"Uh, um," Éduard said, trying to think of how to say what he had to say. "He's dead. Sorry."

"Then it's hopeless." Anthony hung his tiny head.

A fairy, probably the one who had been talking before, flew up and landed on Larthia's hand next to the king. "We demand the right to punish this pixie for his crime," she said.

"We can't allow that," Anthony Oak said. "He's our king."

"And our queen is stuck in that jar, maybe forever."

"Hey," the king said, eyeing the fairy up and down. "You're a ten, baby. Let's get together."

The fairy made a disgusted noise and flew off. The volume of buzzing from the many fairies flying in circles around the vampires went up.

"Éduard," Larthia said. "Maybe you have a connection to Wu Keung's spirit."

"What?" Éduard asked. "Even if I do, so what?"

Anthony Oak turned to look at the vampire. "Why would you have a connection to him?"

Éduard looked embarrassed. "I sort of, well, ate him." Mentioning the eating of the sorcerer made Éduard's hunger bloom. He hadn't had anything since the meal at La Llorona's restaurant.

"Vampires eat flesh?" Oak asked.

"No, not normally. It's a long story."

"Try, dear." Larthia smiled. "Maybe his ghost is one of the ones around us."

Éduard frowned. He didn't want to have a connection to the crazy sorcerer. He felt the weight of the jar on his hand. Anthony Oak stared at him.

The vampire sighed and closed his eyes. He imagined the sorcerer being right in front of him, and how he felt as he consumed the man's flesh. Did he absorb any magic as he did so? he tried to mentally pull the spirit once attached to that flesh toward him.

The jar grew heavier. Éduard opened his eyes and saw a translucent Wu Keung pressing down on the metal lid. "Hi," the sorcerer said.

Larthia gasped. "He's here."

"Turns out being dead makes a necromancer even more powerful. And all those dead humans wandering around are a perfect army. When I control enough of them I will take over this world."

"Can you open the jar?" Éduard asked.

"Sure. I guess I owe you one. But don't expect any mercy when I rule a world of the dead." Wu Keung recited something in Mandarin and took his hand away.

The top of the jar began to turn. Light burst out of it, then the lid flew away and the queen of the fairies came out, rapidly expanding to human size. Her wings spread and supported her in the air. She gave out a great booming laugh and shouted, "I'm free!"

All the fairies moved to fly near their queen. Thousands of their excited, high pitched voices filled the air.

Eduard looked around. The ghost of Wu Keung was gone.

After a minute or two of fairy voices shrieking, the queen leaned over and looked directly at the vampires. She pointed at the pixie king. "There is the miscreant who allowed me to be sealed in that jar!"

"Do I know you?" King Chestnut asked. "I've never met you."

The queen reached down and picked up the pixie royal. "See what you think of it." She placed the king in the jar on Éduard's hand. Chestnut screamed as he shrank into the jar.

The lid magically screwed itself back on. "Take him away," the queen said.

"Yes, ma'am," Anthony Oak said with a smile. "Éduard, please put his highness on the ground, we will load him in one of our vehicles."

The vampire did as he was told. A crew of pixies picked the jar up and carried it away. "How long are you going to leave him in there?"

Oak said, "Just long enough. Put me down too, thank you."

Éduard did, and the pixies got in their vehicles and drove away. When the vampire stood up, the fairy queen stared at him. "Now for you," she said.

"Me? What did I do?"

"You kept your word, you didn't give up, and found a way to free me. The fairies owe you one."

"I don't know what you could do. We're trying to find a way to stop the zombie apocalypse. Do you have any ideas about that?"

The queen looked troubled. Her subjects still flew in circles around her, but they stopped shouting at the top of their tiny lungs. "I am afraid not. Perhaps if I address the gathered crowds of fae, ghosts, and gods, one of them will be able to help."

John Carnahan pushed his way next to Éduard. "What's going on? Who's the flying babe?"

"Shh, she's going to speak," Éduard said.

The queen of the fairies magically magnified her voice. It rang off the face of the nearby museum. "Fairies, ghosts, gods, goblins, monsters, and all who have come to this important meeting, I implore you to think of a way to defeat the hordes of undead and return the human world to normal. The vampires Éduard and Larthia have bravely travelled throughout the city and faced many dangers, and though I was trapped behind glass I witnessed their courage and resourcefulness. They deserve all the help we can give them."

When the speech finished echoing throughout the La Brea Tar Pits, the queen paused to listen to the tumult of ideas that she fully expected would fill the large space.

There was no tumult. She looked hither and yon. So did the vampires. There was, in fact, nobody. All the supernatural creatures were gone.

CHAPTER TWENTY-SIX

"WHERE IS EVERYBODY?" ÉDUARD ASKED.

The plaza in front of the La Brea Tar Pits was empty. The area where tourists gazed through the fence at the oily muck that had spelled doom for many creatures was clear of all activity. The palm trees held their fronds high over nobody.

There was no electric light. The area was dark and made darker by clouds of smoke that billowed over the city. The vampires could see, though even for them it was pretty dark.

The fairy queen flew close to Éduard's face and answered his question. "I don't know."

"What about Gary and Lazarko?" Larthia asked.

The ghost and the werewolf were nowhere to be seen.

Moans could be heard. They were no longer in the fairy world. Zombies were finding their way into the area. "Gary!" Éduard shouted. "Lazarko!"

Out of the night, two figures approached. Both were hairy and had sharp teeth and claws. One wore a nice dress, heels, and carried a large purse. "If you look for my husband," she said, "look no more." She had one hand clasped on the arm of the other wolf.

"Was just helping friends fight zombies," Lazarko said. He looked down at his hairy feet.

"You go away for over a week, no one knows where you are. This is not behavior of proper husband."

"Yes, dear," Lazarko said.

"We are go home. We stay there until this nonsense clears up."

"They're trying to end zombie apocalypse," Lazarko whined. "They need me."

Mrs. Lazarko looked Éduard and Larthia up and down. "What can silly vampires do? Your place is at home. Come along." She started to drag Lazarko away.

Lazarko stood up and made his wife stop. "No. Must help friends."

"They cannot stop zombies!" Mrs. Lazarko said. "Don't be stupid!"

"I am sorry. I will see you at home when it's over."

Mrs. Lazarko let out a low growl, then stalked away.

"Thanks, Lazarko," Éduard said, "but she's right. I think our quest is over."

"Have you seen Gary?" Larthia asked werewolf.

"He find love," Lazarko said and pointed to some bushes. "Over there."

Éduard looked around for the ghost. He heard a different kind of moaning, something that didn't sound like zombies at all.

Larthia smiled. "I think I know what that is." She turned and followed the sound. Next to the stairway that led up to the museum there were some low bushes. The sound came from there, and it was definitely not zombies.

"Oh, ooooh, oooooooooooh," Gary's voice came from the

bushes. Then another voice made grunting noises that came faster and faster, followed by an almost simultaneous shout of satisfaction from both of them.

"Gary found love, all right," Éduard said.

"I don't hear anything." Carnahan leaned forward, with his hand behind one ear. "Is it the ghost?"

"Two ghosts," Éduard said.

Shortly, Gary sat up and his head and torso could be seen above the bushes. He saw the vampires, Carnahan and the fairy queen all looking in his direction. "Hey, can't a ghost have a little privacy?"

Another ghost stood and started pulling up his ecto-plasmic pants. He was a tall, very handsome, and very familiar. Gary stood up next to him. "Guys, this is..."

"Rock Hudson!" Larthia shouted.

Éduard realized that it was the late actor, who had died of AIDS before there was a treatment for the disease. The world found out through this tragic event that Hudson was gay.

"I'm a big fan of *McMillan and Wife*," Larthia said.

"The ghost of Rock Hudson is here, and you're talking about a TV show?" Carnahan asked. "Ask him about his classic romantic comedies with Doris Day."

"Thank you," Hudson said. He straightened out his ghostly jacket and tie. "It's always nice to meet a fan."

"We met while you guys were talking about that jar. I see you got out, queenie."

The fairy queen flew close to Gary. "Maybe you can explain why everyone left, Mr. Ghost?"

Gary looked around. "They did? Well, they were pretty disappointed that it wasn't a party."

"And who told them it was a party?" Éduard asked.

"Ok," Gary said. "My bad. I didn't think you would stand

around talking about a jar. Everyone got bored. I started talking to the other ghosts, and..." he glanced up at Hudson. "...got distracted."

"This is like hearing half of a phone conversation," Carnahan complained. "What were they doing in that bush anyway?"

"What do you think?" Éduard asked.

"Ohhh...ghosts can do that? How, if they aren't solid?"

"We're solid enough," Gary explained, "since we're on the same plane of existence."

Éduard told Carnahan what the ghost said.

"I have to put that in a movie."

The moaning of zombies got closer. "We'd better get John out of here," Éduard said. Of course, if the movie director's usefulness was over he could serve as dinner. The smell of living human was almost overpowering when the director stood near him.

"Everyone in the helicopter," Carnahan said.

"Get to the choppa?" Éduard asked. "I always wanted to say that."

"That wasn't my movie."

"But it was Arnim Blackenovum, who's in some of your movies."

"Then save it for when you see Arnim. Are we going to get to safety?"

The moaning was closer. Éduard saw a lady in a wedding dress that was soaked in blood coming toward them. He stayed close to Carnahan as the group moved toward the helicopter.

"Mr. Carnahan, can you drop us at our condo? I guess we'll hole up there until..." Larthia used her vampire claws to half-sever the neck of a man in a jogging outfit. Blood spurted out of the man's neck and he fell.

"That's no good," Éduard said. "We have no blood there, and the front door was busted in."

"Oh, right." A teenaged boy in shorts and a muscle shirt grabbed Carnahan by the shoulder. Larthia picked him up and threw him over the fence. He landed in the tar with a squoosh, where he would keep company with the prehistoric animals forever.

Éduard opened the back door of the helicopter and waited for Larthia to get in. He then escorted Carnahan around to the pilot's door and helped him in, ignoring the delicious aroma. He had to fight off a very fat woman, decapitating her before the stopped coming at him, then got into the helicopter behind the pilot and pulled the door shut.

Lazarko got into the seat next to Carnahan.

"You sure you don't want to go with your wife?" Éduard asked him.

"Stuck at home with family for who knows how long? I go with you."

Gary came in through the side. "I want to come too."

"Aren't you happy with Rock?"

"He's a movie star, he has lots of ghosts after him."

"Then follow the chopper. I don't know where we're going."

"No one does, do they?" Gary asked. He pulled out of the helicopter.

Carnahan started up the helicopter, lights all around him coming on.

Carnahan started the rotors and the noise filled the cabin. Éduard put on his headset. Zombies pounded on the transparent panels in the doors. The helicopter lifted, but had trouble climbing in the air with the weight of zombies holding onto the skids.

"We're going to my submarine," Carnahan said.

"I'm sorry," Larthia said. "Did you say submarine?"

"Yeah." Carnahan moved the flying machine forward, still dragging a chain of zombies. A few fell off and splattered on the pavement. "I told you I know someone who might be able to help."

"I appreciate everything you've done for us," Éduard said, "but I think you should find some find someplace safe, with other humans."

"There are no zombies where we're going," Carnahan said. The helicopter lifted high in the night sky, still with several bodies clinging to the skids. "I guarantee it."

Éduard's stomach growled, and his hunger for blood flared too. He had to get something to eat soon, or he would attack Carnahan, despite the fact that eating him would make the helicopter crash.

"Are you all right, dear?" Larthia asked.

"Hungry. Very hungry."

"Me too. I haven't had any blood since we ate at Maria's restaurant."

The last zombie fell off as the helicopter turned toward the ocean.

"How about the council chamber?" Larthia asked. "I bet a lot of vampires have gone there. We can decide what to do. Mr. Carnahan, take us to the Hollywood sign."

"No can do," Carnahan said. He continued to fly southwest.

"Where are you taking us?" Éduard demanded.

"You'll see. My friend will help."

"We've talked to fairies, pixies, ghosts, monsters, and

even gods," Éduard said. "No one knows what caused the zombie apocalypse."

"My friend isn't just any god. He's an old god. Some call him Great Old One."

"You're speaking in riddles, man."

"Yes, I am. I just want you to be prepared. We're going to meet one of the oldest beings who dwells on this earth. If anyone knows, he does. When you meet him, you must bow and say a certain phrase."

"What phrase?"

"Ph'nglui mglw'nafh Cthulhu R'lyeh wgah'nagl fhtagn."

CHAPTER TWENTY-SEVEN

THE HELICOPTER FLEW PAST THE COASTLINE AND OUT over the Pacific Ocean. The stars were amazingly bright, with the city dark except for the raging fires.

Lazarko took the opportunity to nap. He was out, and snoring.

Éduard leaned forward. "You're telling me Cthulhu really exists?"

"Yes," Carnahan said over the intercom.

"And the rest of Lovecraft? Dagon? Mi-gos? Shoggoths? The Necronomicon?"

"I can't say for sure. I've tried to find an authentic copy of the Necronomicon, but there are a lot of fakes out there."

"Lovecraft?" Larthia asked. "That strange man from Providence who wrote those silly stories? I didn't like him."

"You met him?" Carnahan said. "I'm jealous."

"Don't be." Éduard shook his head. "He wouldn't even talk to Larthia, he had no use for women or people with brown skin."

"How could a man who spent most of his life in Rhode

Island, and a few years in New York, know about a real god?" Larthia asked.

"Dreams, maybe," Carnahan said. "All I know is that I was exploring the sea bottom in my submarine one day and I went through a cave and came out in R'lyeh."

"The city where Cthulhu lies dreaming," Éduard said.

"Yeah. I got to talk to the big guy. He gets up every millennia or so, to use the bathroom and have a snack."

"I'm surprised the snack wasn't you."

"It almost was, but then he found out who I am. He's a *Dominator* fan."

"Cthulhu watches movies."

"He has a home theater, with a Blu-Ray player and surround sound. He likes to see the world that he will someday destroy."

"Where are we going, Mr. Carnahan?" Larthia asked. The helicopter was over the dark ocean. No lights could be seen.

"You'll see."

"Does Cthulhu ever watch movies about himself? Or other Lovecraft-based movies?"

"He said he liked *Re-Animator,* but none of the sequels."

"I didn't like that," Larthia said. "Éduard and I are animated corpses, and we don't go around decapitating people."

"We just kill them."

"Yes, darling, but without all the mess."

Lights appeared on the horizon. They were attached to an oil rig. The helicopter turned toward it.

"Lovecraft's influence goes a lot further than actual adaptations of his stories," Éduard said. "You can see it in movies like *Hellboy* and *Alien.*"

"I'm sorry," Larthia said. "Give me an old-fashioned

vampire movie, with a dashing romantic hero and a love interest he can turn into a vampire to be by his side forever. Like our story." She touched Éduard on the arm. "Except I turned you. No tentacles and weird stuff."

"Are we going to the oil rig?"

"It was abandoned, it hasn't pumped oil in years," Carnahan said. "I bought it as the base for my sub."

As the helicopter approached the rig, more lights came on, illuminating a landing pad. Éduard could see a man standing near it. Carnahan expertly landed and cut the engine. The rotors slowed down and the noise faded away.

"Nice to see you, sir," a tall man in a red jumpsuit said as Carnahan stepped out of the helicopter.

"Prep the sub, Michaels."

"Yes, sir." Michaels looked toward the vampires as they stepped down. "Can I get you and your guests anything?"

The scent of Michaels hit Éduard hard. He could barely resist grabbing the man and devouring him right there and then.

"They don't need anything, and I want to get going as soon as the sub is ready." Carnahan gestured at a steel stairway that led to a lower level. Michaels started down it.

Éduard caught up with Carnahan and tried to talk quietly. "Do you really need him? He would feed both me and Larthia."

"There's only three people out here, Michaels and his wife and their baby. I'm not going to let you eat any of them."

"With all due respect, human, you couldn't stop me."

"Then you'd never stop the zombie apocalypse."

Éduard cursed internally. He and Larthia had come so far, it made sense to continue the quest. He pushed his hunger and blood lust down. It was getting harder and harder to do so.

Lazarko got out of the helicopter, still looking groggy. "Where is this?"

"There was a head wind," Gary said, floating up the landing pad. "Sorry I'm late."

At the bottom of the ladder a landing led to a door. The machinery of the oil rig towered over the vampires and werewolf as they stepped onto the steel floor. The door opened and a blonde woman came out, holding a two-year old in her arms.

"Mr. Carnahan," the woman said. "We didn't know if we'd see you again. What's happening on the mainland? The satellite TV went out a week ago, but before that they said people were eating each other?"

"It's bad, Lanie. I'm glad your little family is safe out here. Mia is growing fast."

Lanie kissed the toddler on her head. "She had the flu, I was frantic because the Teledoc didn't answer my calls. But she slept all day yesterday and now she's fine."

The little girl turned her gaze to the vampires. Something about her face seemed strange to Éduard. Her eyes didn't move, and she didn't blink.

Larthia must have sensed something was wrong too. "May I hold her?"

Lanie hesitated, then nodded. Larthia reached her arms out. Before she could take the baby, little Mia leaned into her mother's right arm and bit hard.

Lanie screamed. Blood ran down her arm. Mia pulled back, taking a piece of flesh with her. Her little jaw worked as she chewed.

"I tried to save her," Larthia said.

"I know." Éduard put his arm around her.

Carnahan swore. "Let's go." He pushed open the metal door and led the vampires and Lazarko into the interior of the rig. The metal door closed and locked, and Gary came through it a moment later. "Sure leave me out there with the zoms," he said. They worked their way down, through areas filled with machinery and then a cozy living area.

A final climb down a ladder brought them to a platform, where a small submarine rested. Michaels stood nearby. "All ready to go, Mr. Carnahan."

"Thanks. Carnahan took three steps up and opened the hatch on top of the sub. He lowered himself inside. Éduard and Larthia followed. Just as in the helicopter, Lazarko had shotgun.

"Can I eat him now?" Éduard asked. "He's going to be one of those things soon."

Carnahan pulled the hatch shut and turned the wheel. "Not if he finds someplace to hide. We'll pick him up on the way back."

Gary came in and hovered in front of the two vampires. "I have to float through water now?" he asked.

"You won't drown, will you?" Éduard asked.

"No, but it feels weird." Gary sighed. "A ghost's gotta do what a ghost's gotta do." He left the interior of the submarine.

A large round window in front of the movie director showed the world outside the tiny sub. The interior space was smaller than the inside of a Volkswagen Beetle.

The air filled with the smell of a living, delicious human. Éduard had to control himself as he strapped his seatbelt on. "So it's true," he said.

"What's true?" Carnahan asked as he started the engine. The sound filled the space, so he had to raise his voice.

"Those people have not been on the mainland since the

zombie plague started. But the baby still turned when it died from the flu."

Carnahan pushed a control forward and the sub began to descend. It hit the water with a bump. "That's classic Romero," the movie director said. "People turn when they die, even if they aren't bitten."

"Why does reality so slavishly copy fiction? I expected at least some of the details to be different than in the movies."

The water line got higher and higher in the window, until the sub was under. The light turned a murky green.

"I love movies," Carnahan said. He made the little sub move forward. "But reality does have surprises that no one could write in a script. That's why I like to actually dive into the ocean, not just make movies about it."

Éduard leaned back in his seat. He had a lot to think about.

The submarine descended, following the sloping bottom of the continental shelf. Swarms of fish surrounded the sub then moved away. A shark poked its nose curiously at the window but seemed to find it uninteresting.

"How long will it take?" Larthia asked.

"A few hours," Carnahan replied. "Just sit back and relax."

"You do realize you have two hungry vampires right behind you?" Larthia rubbed Éduard's shoulder, as if willing him to stay strong.

"Hungry vampires who don't know how to drive the sub," Carnahan said. "But I'll go as fast as I can. There are people down there."

"Really? Who?"

"Cthulhu cultists. Some Dagon followers too. Deep Ones. R'lyeh is a city, someone has to live there other than the god."

"I like seafood," Éduard said. Larthia laughed.

More than an hour later, they were deep enough that there was very little life in the water. The view out the window showed mainly floating bits of unknown detritus.

At one point Gary came to the front window and stuck his tongue out. Éduard and Larthia laughed.

"What's so funny?" Carnahan asked.

"Gary's out there, goofing around."

The sub moved forward. Lazarko had resumed his nap.

It was dark enough, with only the instruments on the panel in front of the driver illuminating the interior, that Éduard felt himself going into vampire slumber. He glanced at Larthia. She was still, corpselike.

Before he succumbed, Éduard managed to say, "Hours of floating through the ocean. If this was a movie, it would cut to –"

CHAPTER TWENTY-EIGHT

"THERE IT IS!"

Éduard jerked awake and hit his head on the ceiling of the tiny sub. "Ow!"

"There's what?" Larthia asked, also waking from slumber, but more gently.

Lazarko kept snoring.

"The entrance to R'lyeh." Carnahan pointed at an unassuming cave entrance in a rock wall.

"That's just a cave." Éduard rubbed his head.

"That's a cave, but not just a cave." Carnahan steered the submarine into the rocky opening. Complete blackness surrounded the little vehicle, except for its headlights shining and showing nothing.

"I don't see anything."

"Wait for it." As the movie director finished that sentence, a tiny amount of light began to appear outside.

Hunger rumbled through Éduard's necrotic innards. He hoped there really were people in the sunken city.

Fairly soon the light from above became brighter.

Carnahan directed the sub upwards. Before too long it broke through the surface of a large lagoon inside the cave.

"Where are we?" Éduard asked.

"The docking bay. A surprising number of subs come here to trade with the city, or bring people in and out."

"Lazarko!" Éduard said, shaking the werewolf's shoulder. Wake up."

"Huh? What? Am I home in Leningrad?"

"What's that huge sub?" Larthia pointed to the left. A very large submarine was docked along the wall. It had an unusual design. It didn't look like it was military, American or Soviet or any other.

"The Seaview." Carnahan steered toward a set of docks. "Its last adventure was when it found R'Lyeh in 1968. It's been here ever since."

"You mean *Voyage to the Bottom of the Sea* was real?" Éduard asked.

"The show was a re-creation, but the sub was real and the episodes were based on things that really happened."

"What about *Lost in Space*?"

"I don't know."

"*Land of the Giants?*"

"I only know about the Seaview."

"*H.R. Pufnstuf?*"

"Maybe. There are rumors. We're here." Carnahan took off his seatbelt and got up, stooping to stay under the ceiling. He took hold of the ring that opened the door and turned it. The seal popped open and the smell of salt water filled the tiny sub.

Carnahan pushed himself up and was out of the sub. Éduard stood, his head rising through the hatch. He couldn't see much, it was a large area lit by too few electric lights.

He jumped up with vampire strength and landed on the wooden dock. Carnahan was tying a rope to the metal thing that people tie ropes to on docks. Larthia landed next to him after her own jump.

Lazarko clambered out of the sub and jumped to the dock. "Not like here. Has bad smell."

A spout of water appeared next to the dock. Gary came out of it and spread his arms wide. "I'm here and I'm fabulous!" He shook himself and water sprayed all over. "There's water in places I haven't felt since I had a body."

"Looks like Marina Del Rey, if it was in a dank cave."

Éduard laughed. "And no boats, just subs."

"This way," Carnahan called out. He walked toward the buildings on shore.

"He's going pretty fast. Is he trying to avoid being eaten?" Larthia said.

The two vampires, ghost and werewolf followed the movie director. "I really do need to find food," Éduard said. "I don't know what happens when a vampzom goes too long between meals, but I think we're about to find out."

"Do you really think you're a vampzom, dear? I was hoping that finding the cure to the zombie apocalypse would cure you, too."

"What I am is starving, and I would eat blood, flesh, or both, and in large quantities."

The architecture of the city loomed above them as they left the dock area. It was built for inhabitants vastly larger than humans, and with unknowable anatomies. Windowless slabs of buildings, and curved structures that were at one moment concave and at the next convex. Éduard's mind rebelled as he tried to make sense of it all. Everything was a dark green, as if covered with mold.

"First time I was here," Carnahan said, "I just curled up

in a ball and refused to look. The non-Euclidian geometry is just too much."

"I always thought Lovecraft just made up that phrase. It didn't seem possible."

"Cthulhu must have conveyed the concept to Lovecraft in his dreams," Carnahan said.

"Explains *Betty Boop* cartoons," Éduard said. "Some of the weirdest shit ever put on film."

"You don't usually curse, Éduard."

"No, my love, but it's the only way to describe some of the work of the Fleischer brothers."

Carnahan pointed forward. "It gets a little better in human town."

The group rounded a corner and saw a small settlement that Euclid would have been much more comfortable with. A smattering of stores and dwellings, made of driftwood, rocks, and detritus from the world above the waves, including plastic bottles and products from shipping containers that fell off their ships.

Human forms, dressed in clothing from many different countries, seaweed, and random bits of cloth, moved around the little town.

"There's a Starbucks down here?" Éduard asked as he looked at the familiar mermaid logo above a doorway.

"Things shift in weird ways, even in human town," Carnahan said. "Look again."

"Now it's a Tea Leaf and Coffee Bean."

"As long as I can get a cup of joe, I don't worry about the sign over the door. Hey Ralph!" Carnahan waved at a pale-skinned man wearing nothing but boxer shorts. Ralph waved back. "He's a deep one who got so deep he ended up here."

"Are these the humans I can eat?"

Carnahan shook his head. "I have a much better meal in mind."

"Better serve it up soon, or I will just grab the first human I see and chow down."

The vampires followed the movie director through the winding streets of human town. Lazarko gaped at the strange scenery like a tourist in New York. They passed people with fish-like skin, others of every human variety that had somehow ended up in this impossible place. A few seem to have gone mad because of the shifting unreality around them..

The human structures gave way to an open plaza, constructed at angles that didn't seem possible. "This way," Carnahan said. He led them to a wall with an elaborate doorway in it, decorated with carvings of creatures whose physical details made Éduard and Larthia look away, and tall enough to admit a *Star Wars* walker.

"This is a big gate," Lazarko said.

"Thanks, we never would have noticed without your keen intellect to figure it out," Gary said.

"If I could..."

"Touch me, you'd tear me apart. If I had a lover for every time you have said that, I would never stop having sex."

"This is the holiest place in the city," Carnahan said. "Within sleeps the oldest of the old ones, the most powerful of the gods that ruled the Earth before the earliest ancestors of mankind looked up at the sky and wondered what the fuck was going on."

"Oh no you don't!" a voice shouted.

Éduard saw a plump man in an elaborate costume that had a stiff, tall protrusion behind his head. Fake tentacles were sewn onto the costume and stuck out in all directions. Several more figures, men and women, in similar costumes but without the tentacles, walked behind the tentacled man.

Carnahan bowed deeply. "Your holiness."

"Don't 'your holiness' me, Carnahan." The costumed man snapped. "I told you never to come back here. HE told me to kill you on sight."

The other priests, Éduard guessed that's what they were, arrayed themselves in a way that completely blocked the entrance.

"I'm sure HE was just feeling a little grumpy." Carnahan straightened up and smiled. "He's changed his mind by now, I'm sure."

"The mighty Cthulhu hasn't changed his mind in all the eons of existence that he has waited to regain the surface and destroy all humans, and you know it."

Éduard felt his hunger swell up and fill his being. The priests seemed like nothing but a buffet, arranged before him in an appetizing display. He felt Larthia touch his arm. Her eyes showed she too felt more than a little peckish.

"And who are these? More humans?" The main priest asked. "HE will not see them. HE is sound asleep and I have instructions not to wake him until the next season of *Ash vs. The Evil Dead* drops on Netflix."

Carnahan laughed. "I'm sorry, your holiness, but that show has been canceled."

"WHAT?" The priests eyes went round. A groan went through the ranks of the other priests. "HE will not be pleased. Still, you may not pass. Go back to the surface and make another crappy movie."

Carnahan turned to the vampires. "There is only one way to get past them."

Éduard, almost drooling from the smell of so much food, knew what the director meant. "Really? Can I?"

"Mangia, my friend."

The head priest looked back and forth between the director and the vampires. "What are you talking about?" He screamed as two vampires came at him with all their preternatural speed. Éduard took the man's head in his hands and took a satisfying bite out of his cheek. The flesh came away like the peel of a juicy orange.

Larthia saw that Éduard had the head priest under control and went for one of the others. It was a woman who had maintained a haughty look as she watched the proceedings, but who changed it to shocked horror as an ancient vampire slashed her jugular vein and drank deeply of the red fountain that sprayed out.

Most of the priests were able to run away, but the two where were caught gave their lives to be the long-delayed meal of the two vampires. The head priest was little more than a skeleton with scraps of meat clinging to it by the time Éduard sank to his knees and gave out a giant burp.

"I am a werewolf, and I eat more neatly than that."

Gary said, "Yeah, that's a sight I will remember for the rest of eternity."

"You can keep that suit," John Carnahan said. "Same to you with my ex-wife's outfit, Larthia."

Éduard was so happy to be full of meat and blood that he had to think for a second. He remembered he was still wearing clothing that Carnahan had loaned him. He looked down. The suit was ruined, covered in blood that dripped off of it, like a wet swimming suit.

"Now, let's go see the big guy."

Getting to his feet, Éduard glanced at his wife. She stood and smiled sheepishly. "I haven't eaten that well for a long time."

"You look like something out of a horror movie," Éduard said. Larthia was almost as bloody as he was.

"I am something out of a horror movie." She followed the movie director.

The doorway led to a dark tunnel. Only an occasional torch on the wall gave it any light. Just as the tunnel seemed to be endless, it opened up into a larger chamber, that was lit by electric lights.

Centered in the room was a bed that could accommodate a blue whale, the largest species of animal that ever existed, if blue whales slept in beds. Lying with blankets covering it was a form that was both repulsive and familiar. Tentacles flopped from one side of the stupendous head to another as the Great Old One turned over in his sleep.

"What do we do now? Just wait for him to wake up?" Éduard asked.

Carnahan said, "I'm not sure. Maybe there's an eldritch clock radio."

"What did you do before?" Larthia asked.

"The priests woke him up."

"Excuse me," a voice came from behind them. "Can I help you?"

Éduard turned and saw a human in a nice suit with a blue tie. He was well built, and pleasing to the eye. You could even say he was beautiful.

"It's Mr. Dreamy," Gary said. "Where have you been?"

"William?" Larthia said.

CHAPTER TWENTY-NINE

"YOU HAVE TO BE KIDDING," ÉDUARD SAID.

"It's me," William said. "I'm so glad to see you, Éduard and Larthia. Even you, Lazarko and Gary."

"What happened to you?" Larthia asked. "You were gone the night after we met the hopping vampires."

"I'm so sorry." William smiled a beautiful smile. "I went out to look around, since I don't sleep and zombies can't harm me. I met up with a friendly djinn, and –"

"I'm sorry, a genie?" Éduard asked. "Did it give you three wishes?"

"A djinn," William said. "They don't grant wishes. This one was upset about the zombie apocalypse too."

"Of course it was. And it flew you to Agraba so you two could discuss things over fresh figs and camel burgers."

"Let him speak, Éduard," Larthia said sharply. "We've met some pretty unusual characters ourselves."

Éduard folded his arms and shut up.

"We flew all over the world, trying to find what caused the zombie apocalypse and how to stop it. I'm afraid by the time I got back you were gone. I see you're all right."

"No thanks to you," Éduard said. "Wu Keung tried to enslave us, I had to e – er, kill him, and we've been slogging through zombie guts for well over a week since then. We could have used a super duper vampire with no weaknesses."

"You look like you've killed recently." William came closer.

"Yes, well, we had to get past the priests."

"I see. I really wish I had been with you to help. But the djinn finally told me that only the oldest being on Earth could help me." He gestured toward the huge bed. "Unfortunately I haven't been able to wake him up."

"How did you get to the bottom of the ocean?" Éduard asked.

"I swam, of course."

Éduard rolled his eyes. "Of course. A swimming vampire. Why not?"

"Who is this human behind you?"

"John Carnahan." He held out his hand. "And you are?"

"The movie director?" William smiled broadly. "I really loved *Dominator 2*."

"He's a vampire from those movies where they sparkle," Éduard said.

"Ah," Carnahan said. "I haven't had a chance to see those."

A huge groan filled the enormous chamber. Mighty Cthulhu rolled over. The vampires and Carnahan backed up. One mighty eye opened.

"Fuck," Cthulhu said, his voice deeper than zen. He tossed his blanket off and put his feet on the floor. "Used to be able to sleep through a millennium. Now I gotta pee every two hundred years."

The eternal god stood, towering over Éduard and the

others. He was stark naked. He walked toward one wall, where there was a cyclopean door. He had wings that seemed absurdly small for his size.

Eduard looked horrified and turned his face away.

"I was looking at his wings," Larthia said. "What did you see?"

"Non-Euclidean genitals." Éduard shuddered.

"Really?" Gary asked. "How big?"

"Too big for you, Gary."

Gary shrugged. "I'd give it a shot."

It was only a minute before the door opened and the mighty Cthulhu returned. He was now wearing a fuzzy white robe. He came to the side of the bed and looked down. Each foot was the size of an Airstream trailer.

"Do I see humans at my bedside?" the god rumbled. "Where are my priests?"

Éduard was about to speak but William shouted over him. "I'm sorry, your godliness, your priests ran away."

The god turned and sat on the bed. He peered down at the small group. His tentacles writhed, making his head appear to be an angry octopus. "And why did they do that?"

Éduard stepped forward. "We are vampires, your majesticness. We sort of, ate two of them."

"Vampires. People dream about them but I didn't know they were real."

"We are, and we are on a quest."

"What quest?" Cthulhu asked.

"Larthia and I are determined to find a way to stop the zombie apocalypse."

"The what now?"

"Zombie apocalypse? Have you had any dreams about walking corpses eating people?"

Cthulhu paused. "Well, things seem to be unusually

chaotic up there." He shook his mighty, tentacled head. "No, you can't tell me zombies are real too. I need to stop watching *Z Nation* on SYFY at three a.m."

"It is all true, your godliness." Éduard tried to think of a way to convince the Lovecraftian horror.

"No no no. Out. All of you. I'm going back to bed." Just as he said that, Cthulhu's eyes widened and he sat back on the bed. His tentacles writhed.

The vampires turned and saw the former priests, the woman with blood drenching her robes and the Head Priest, little more than bone, meat, and scraps of clothing, enter the bedchamber. Their jaws worked and they held their arms in front of them. They moaned in a typical zombie fashion.

"Come on," Chthulhu said. "Really? How do you kill them?"

"You have to destroy their brains, sir, um, your eldritch horrorness," Éduard said.

The zombies came toward Éduard and Larthia, then hesitated. Whatever sense told them who was food and who was not made them turn away and lurch toward Carnahan.

The move director backed up. "Someone want to take these two out?"

Lazarko transformed into wolf form and got ready to kill the zombies. Before he could, a huge green ichor-dripping foot slammed down on the former priests, mashing them to jelly on the stone floor. "That should do it," Cthulhu said. "Now, let's get more comfortable."

In the blink of an eye, the god appeared in a smaller form, between six and seven feet tall, still wearing the robe. "Easier to talk to humans this way."

"You can shrink?" Larthia asked.

"I'm not made of normal matter. I can appear in many ways."

"Great Cthulhu," Carnahan said.

"Now you're my size," Gary said. "Rrrrrrow."

"I'm not talking to you, ghost. And who is this other? A shapeshifter?"

"I am a werewolf," Lazarko said with great dignity as his suit and jewelry reappeared.

"Bah. Give me shoggoths. They can turn into useful things. Who needs a wolf?"

"Is not need. Is want."

Gary chimed in, "I used to date a bear, but that's a whole different animal."

"Vampires?" Cthulhu said. "Why are you here?"

Éduard said, "We are hoping to find a way to end the zombie plague."

Cthulhu growled deeply and waggled his tentacles. He flapped his wings, which were clearly not big enough to allow him to fly anywhere. The vampires looked puzzled.

"You guys aren't scared of me at all?"

"Um," Éduard started to say, but Cthulhu interrupted him.

"Not feeling like you might go mad at the mere sight of me?"

"You are very intimidating," Larthia, trying to sooth the god. "But your image is so common in the world, we've gotten used to it."

"It's the stuffed toys, isn't it?" Cthulhu asked. "And they put me in an episode of *South Park* Without even calling my agent!"

"I'm afraid you are in public domain," Éduard explained. "No one needs to ask permission."

Cthulhu shook his fearsome head. "Should have gone

up and destroyed the world when I could make some money off it. Anyway, what were you saying?"

"The zombie apocalypse," Éduard said. "Is there any way to stop it?"

"Do you know what started it?"

"We thought maybe there was some radiation from space, like in *Night of the Living Dead*," Larthia offered.

"Or a virus," Éduard said. "That's a popular explanation."

"Government experiments," Carnahan put in. "Barrels of chemicals, like in *Return of the Living Dead*."

"I travelled with a djinn who thought it might be some evil magic," William said.

"No, no," Cthulhu said. "This sort of thing usually happens because people want it."

Éduard hesitated, then said, "What?"

"I see the dreams of billions of people. If enough human brains concentrate on one thing, they can make it happen."

Éduard laughed. Cthulhu turned his fearsome gaze on the vampire, tentacles writhing. "Do you mock me?"

"No, no of course not. It's just, that's ridiculous. People can't think things into existence."

"No? Vampires have seen a major change in themselves because of the power of the human mind."

"What do you mean?"

"Think back, both of you. I sense the male, Éduard, is it? That Éduard is young compared to his companion. But both lived for some time before storytelling on film began."

"I am ancient," Larthia said, "From the Etruscan civilization that gave rise to Rome."

"I'm just a baby, as you said." Éduard said. "Compared to Larthia at least. But what does that have to do with anything?"

"Did you always hide from sunlight, finding darkness in which to sleep between the first sliver of dawn and the last rays of sunset?"

"Of course." Éduard looked at Larthia, who nodded. "That's what vampires do."

"Think very hard," the ancient god said.

Éduard furrowed his brow. What could Cthulhu be suggesting? He searched his memories. He had always slept during the day. Going out in sunlight would mean bursting into flame. Right? Of course.

Larthia came to him, a strange look on her face. "Darling...I think...maybe..."

Scenes of walking through London, Larthia on his arm, he in top hat and tails, she in a skirt that brushed the ground, daylight showing everything around him, pushed their way into his mind.

"Remember Prague?" Larthia whispered. "We left America during the civil war and toured Europe. I think we walked in the sun."

"That can't be." But it was. Memories now flooded Éduard's brain.

"What happened? Why didn't we even remember it?" Larthia asked the elder god.

"*Nosferatu*," Cthulhu said. "They needed a low budget ending, so they invented the idea that dawn kills vampires."

"No, no," Éduard tried to make sense of this, tried to remember hiding during the day before the unauthorized German film version of *Dracula* was released. But he couldn't. He had just been assuming that his life had always involved fear of the sun.

"Not that many people saw *Nosferatu*," Cthulhu continued, "Bram Stoker's wife sued and tried to have all prints destroyed. But other movie writers picked up the idea until it was standard."

"How can you know all this?" William asked. "You haven't been on the surface since before humans existed."

"Dreams," the god said. "Very powerful stuff. When enough people dream about the same thing for a long time, well, it can happen."

"Can I say something?" Carnahan said.

"What?" Great Cthulhu turned toward the move director.

"This makes sense to me. I'm in the business of creating mass dreams. I know a lot of people want to live on the alien moon where *Examplar* takes place, or find romance on a doomed ship."

"So you're saying," Éduard tried to put his jumbled thoughts in order, "that millions of humans are coming back to life and eating living humans, destroying their civilization in the process, because they WANT that to happen?"

Cthulhu shrugged. "Pretty much."

CHAPTER THIRTY

THIS REVELATION MADE ÉDUARD VERY SAD. THAT humans would be so obsessed with popular monsters that they caused their own destruction. His shoulders sagged. "Then there's nothing we can do."

"I don't believe," Lazarko growled. "People are stupid, yes, but to cause the end of themselves?"

"Nuclear war, climate change, biological weapons," Gary said. "Not to mention the *Fast and Furious* franchise."

"You make point," Lazarko had to concede.

Larthia put her arm around Éduard's shoulders and held him tight. "I'm sorry," she said. "I know how much you wanted to find an answer."

"Nothing to do but go home and starve." Éduard sighed.

"Well," William said.

The vampires looked at the sparkly vampire.

"There might be one thing."

"What?" Carnahan asked.

"If zombies weren't so popular..."

"It's too late!" Éduard exclaimed. "Almost all humans are infected!"

Cthulhu shook his head. "What are you suggesting, vampire?"

"I've been exploring R'lyeh for several days. I have talked to many people and other creatures. There are rumors about something that could help."

"I don't know what you're talking about." The eldritch deity tried to look innocent, but clearly he knew something.

"They call it the time pool."

Conversation stopped. The vampires gaped. Carnahan laughed.

"No such thing. Well, nice meeting you all. Have a nice trip home."

William smiled. "I know where it is, your godliness. It's deep in the caverns behind this chamber. I have walked them all, waiting for you to wake up. I saw the door behind which it must lurk."

"Oh, all right. If it will get you out of here. Besides, it's my job to destroy the human world, I don't want to go up there and find everyone already dead."

Eduard tried to figure out how any of this made sense. "Time pool? Are you talking about time travel? To when?"

"You tell me. Figure out the exact moment that would make zombies unpopular."

Larthia raised her eyebrows. "I don't even know when to suggest."

"Got it," Carnahan said. "You have to make sure that *Night of the Living Dead* is never made."

"I really love that movie," Éduard said. "It's a brilliant use of a shoestring budget. It was scary as hell in its time. It launched Romero and his friends on great careers."

"Me too," Carnahan said. "But it's either that or the zombie apocalypse for real."

"Do you have a time and place?" Great Cthulhu asked.

"Pittsburgh, before they started to make the movie," Éduard said. "1967? '66? I don't know exactly where they lived."

Cthulhu closed his eyes and seemed to be thinking. "I see everything, past present and future. Give me a sec. Got it. Okay, this way to the time pool." He strode toward the back of his bedroom.

"Do you think he's really going to send us back in time?" Éduard asked Carnahan as they followed the tentacled figure.

"I never heard him say he could do that before, but he is an elder god."

There was a tunnel in the back of the chamber. It was not protected by the door, just by part of the wall covering it. Cthulhu led the vampires, werewolf, ghost and Carnahan through a number of twists and turns. Éduard couldn't have found the way out if he needed to.

A small cave opened up, in the center of which was a bubbling pool. Pockets of a black substance swelled up and burst, releasing a foul-smelling mist. Cthulhu stood over it and waved his hands. "It's set. All you have to do is jump in."

The vampires and the movie director walked toward the pool. "Not you, Carnahan. I'll escort you to your sub."

"What?" Carnahan said.

"He's been with us for a while," Éduard said.

" All who use the time pool will not return." Cthulhu looked very serious. "After you change time you will live in the new reality."

"Relive the sixties through the nineties, and into the twenty first century?" Larthia wondered.

"We can see Hair on Broadway again." Éduard said. "Invest in Apple. Go to Burning Man before it became commercialized, and bury our victims in the desert."

239

"Darling, you make it sound so romantic." Larthia and Éduard held hands.

"We'll meet up at a bar in Westwood and have a laugh over the whole adventure," Larthia said to Carnahan.

"Uh, okay. Here's to the return of civilization!" Carnahan stepped back.

"What about us?" Gary asked.

"I go," Lazarko said. "Want to see end of this."

"All right," the ghost said. "All for one, one for all."

"I do not know if your substance will travel through the time sludge," Cthulhu said.

"I made it through hundreds of mile of Pacific ocean."

The god shrugged. "Very well, you may try."

"I'm going to stay," William said. "I'm immortal, I'll watch over Cthulhu while he sleeps. You do need a new head priest, right big guy?"

"I suppose. Now, are you four going?"

Larthia whispered in Éduard's ear. "Can we trust him?"

"Trust a god whose one goal is the destruction of all human life? Why not?"

"No real life for us in a zombie apocalypse, I suppose."

Eduard held out his hand. Larthia grasped it firmly. They took two steps and jumped, followed by a werewolf and a ghost.

CHAPTER THIRTY-ONE

THERE WAS NO SENSATION OF SINKING INTO THE noxious pool. There was no wrenching transition. Éduard and Larthia found themselves in a hallway. A normal, ordinary, not very clean hallway.

Either by virtue of time travel or something Cthulhu did, their clothes, which they had borrowed from Carnahan, were neat and free of bloodstains.

They stood in front of a door. A normal, ordinary door.

Éduard decided that if you are standing in front of a door, the obvious thing to do is to knock on it. A moment after he did so, the door opened. A young man stood there. "Yeah?" he said.

"We're uh, looking for some filmmakers."

The young man looked surprised. "We're planning a film."

"May we come in?" Larthia asked, then walked past the young man into the room. Éduard followed her. Lazarko also entered the room, closing the door behind him.

Gary came through the door. "What a dump," he said.

Two more young men sat on a couch. The couch had

seen better days. There was a coffee table in the center of the room. One of the young men wore a beard, and he had his feet up on the coffee table.

"Who are you?" the young man with the beard asked.

"I am Éduard, and this is Larthia and Lazarko. We are..." he wasn't sure what to say next. Then he had an idea. "Talent scouts from Hollywood."

"Yes," Larthia said. "We heard you had talent." She leaned over and whispered into Éduard's ear. "I thought we were just going to eat them."

"Not this time, dear one," Éduard whispered back. "They will contribute a lot to American culture, they need to live." Then he turned to the young man with the beard. "George Romero."

"Yeah. What's this all about?"

"John Russo," Éduard said, not sure which one would reply.

"That's me," the young man who had answered the door said.

"You must be Russell Streiner," Éduard said to the third young man, who had a beer can in his hand. The label said "Iron City."

More beer cans of the same brand littered the surface of the coffee table.

"How did you hear about us?" Romero asked. "We make commercials. Mostly for local products."

"It was..." Éduard tried to think. A factoid from the internet jumped into his brain. A well-known TV show was also shot in Pittsburgh at this time. Romero and his crew had shot segments for it.

"...Mr. Rogers Gets a Tonsillectomy. Brilliant cinema. My partners and I were very impressed."

The jaws of all three of the young men dropped. "Nobody knows that was us," Romero said.

"Word gets around, young man. We are prepared to invest in your careers. You're planning a feature?"

"We want to do some really gory horror," Russo said. "I have an idea about ghouls who eat people."

"I just read *I Am Legend*," Romero said. "Something like that."

"Is stupid idea," Lazarko said.

"Don't mind Mr. Lazarko," Éduard said.

"Is that a Russian accent?" Russo said. "Is he a communist spy?"

"He's our investor," Éduard quickly said. "He has a few million he wants he doesn't want to pay taxes on."

"A few million fleas in his fur is more like it," Gary said.

Lazarko glared at the ghost, making the young men look puzzled because they couldn't see Gary.

Éduard paced back and forth and stroked his chin. He tried to look like a Hollywood insider. He turned his back on the young men and gestured to Larthia to join him.

"What are you thinking?" Larthia whispered.

"The best way to ruin their careers," Éduard whispered, "is to give them careers. Seduce them with money. Have them work on forgettable crap and pay them so much they can't afford to do anything really creative."

Turning back to the young men, Éduard said, "I'm familiar with that Legend book. It's been done. Besides, vampires are played out."

"What's your budget?" Larthia asked.

"We've put together six thousand dollars. We're going to do it in black and white to save money."

Larthia let out a laugh. "That wouldn't cover craft services for one day on our projects."

"If we can come up with a great concept, I mean really great," Éduard said, "Mr. Lazarko is prepared to fund you at two million."

Streiner had been standing next to the couch. His legs gave way and he sat on the arm of the dilapidated piece of furniture. Romero and Russo gasped.

"Aha!" Éduard shouted dramatically. "I have it!"

"This will be good," Larthia said. "Éduard is a genius."

"You want ghouls? You want cannibals? I give you..."

The young men hung on every word.

"Aardvarks!"

The room fell silent. "Night of the, dead, no, living, no, living dead aardvarks!"

"Um, Mr...Edward?" George Romero asked. "That seems kind of, well, silly."

Éduard could see that Larthia was trying not to laugh. "Believe me, Éduard's ideas always make money. He makes it rain."

"What does rain have to do with it?" Streiner asked.

Larthia waved her hand. "Money! It will pour down on you!"

"Can I talk with my friends for a second?" Romero asked.

"Of course, of course."

The young men huddled up across the room, their backs to the vampires.

"Do we have two million dollars?" Larthia asked in a low voice.

"Money is never a problem for us," Éduard said. "Just drink the blood of someone who has it and reinvest it in ourselves." Then his vampire hearing picked up something that Russo said in the huddle.

"We make one two-million-dollar movie with this idiot,

we can write our own tickets. We can make the ghoul movie after that. In color."

Not with the onerous contracts I'll make you sign, Éduard thought. *Night of the Living Dead* will never be made, never inspire sequels and spinoffs and comic books and TV shows and video games. Never create a real zombie apocalypse through the will of the people.

The young men turned around to face the vampires.

"So what'll it be, boys?" He held out his hand. "Deal?"

George Romero glanced at his friends, then shook Éduard's hand. "Deal."

CHAPTER THIRTY-TWO

ÉDUARD DODGED PIKACHU, SIDE-STEPPED OPTIMUS Prime, and almost collided with the late Charles Manson. Larthia was somewhere in the crowd, they had both gone out to see the night, again, when it all started. They had stocked plenty of blood ahead of time. They could have stayed at home, but they felt like going out to experience the West Hollywood Halloween Street Party in all its crowded glory.

After living through the end of the sixties, the seventies, eighties, nineties, oughts, and teens, they had returned to the moment when the zombie apocalypse had made itself known to Éduard. This time, there were no zombies. Zombies weren't a thing, they had never been invented, unless you counted the old Voodoo zombie movies.

Éduard laughed when he saw a living dead aardvark in the crowd. They had done surprisingly well, and there were two sequels, each cheaper than the last. But they weren't a pop culture icon.

George Romero had gotten sick of Hollywood and returned to Pittsburgh. He made *Martin*, *Knightriders*, and

Monkey Shines. He did all right. So did his friends, they became writers and directors on a variety of Hollywood projects. Even their friend Duane Jones had a modest career, becoming one of the first black action heroes.

Éduard and Larthia had realized sometime in the seventies that this wasn't their original universe. Éduard chalked it up to the grandfather paradox. If you go back in time to solve a problem, then the problem doesn't happen and you have no motivation to go back in time. They clearly had created a new universe. They tried not to think about what was still happening in their universe of origin.

The new universe had not contained any other version of themselves, so they didn't have to worry about that. Also, Éduard was only a vampire, he had no desire for flesh. His only theory about that was that zombies didn't exist in this world so he couldn't be one.

The vampires still couldn't go out in sunlight, this universe did have *Nosferatu*.

They had thought of contacting John Carnahan when he appeared on the scene, to see if he remembered them. It turned out that he was named James Cameron in this universe, and his movies were *The Terminator*, *Titanic,* and *Avatar*. Clearly not the man they knew.

"Smile," Gary said as he zipped his ghostly form past Éduard. "It's a party!" Gary was happy wherever there were gay people. He had spent the last few decades finding his fantasy lovers that he had missed the first time.

"Is too crowded," Lazarko said. In werewolf form, he was just another person in costume. He had missed his wife for a while. In this universe she was married to an American film distributor. Eventually Lazarko found a new wife in the Russian community.

"Enjoy it, Laz," Éduard said. "We are back at the

beginning!"

"I know. The night it started. I will miss not knowing future, and how stock market goes." Lazarko had become very rich investing in things like Microsoft and Google.

Over the noise of the crowd, and bands playing, Éduard was still able to find Larthia. They joined hands. She wore a Morticia Addams dress, in which she looked ravishing. They were entering a new time in their long lives, and the future was unknown. It felt good. They smiled at each other, happy that they had actually done it, they had defeated the zombie apocalypse, if only in one universe.

The screaming started down the street, and flashed through the crowd. People began running, or trying to. They tripped over each other, leaving piles of costumed bodies on the pavement.

Éduard looked toward the direction where the screaming had begun. It couldn't be zombies, he thought. He couldn't see anything. A huge sound filled the world, beating at his ears and filling his brain with fear.

He clutched Larthia's hand and they both looked up. Even though the sky was dark they could see a darker shape, with flashing lights all over it. It was bigger than West Hollywood itself.

Hatches opened and nightmare things with seven legs descended. The things landed and started using energy rays on the crowd.

Éduard and Larthia got to the edge of the street and cowered against a building. A woman in a Scrubbing Bubbles costume was blasted into pieces in front of them. A small section of her landed on the lapel of Éduard's Anne Rice vampire outfit.

"Don't say it, dear," Larthia said.

"We..." Éduard said. "We have to stop the alien invasion!"

ABOUT THE AUTHOR

ROBIN REEED lives in Southern California because writers are supposed to live there. She has the requisite number of writer's cats. Robin writes humor, science fiction, horror and thrillers.

facebook.com/RobinRM

twitter.com/rrreed94

OTHER BOOKS BY ROBIN REED

Xanthan Gumm

Powers vs. Power (Books 1 – 3)

'Twas the Night

Beer, Cats, and the Future of Civilization

God, Monsters, and Antigrav Underwear